CW00401002

Ambush in Purgatory

The renegades had hit three Army posts. All they took were guns and ammunition: until the last raid. That time they got away with a Gatling gun. Now, somewhere out there, was a gang with enough firepower to take on the United States Army. Find them, the Justice Department told Angel. And stop them.

What they didn't know was that out in the empty, lawless land, every trigger-happy gunslick in the territory had been given the word: when you see him coming, trap Angel. And kill him.

Ambush in Purgatory

Daniel Rockfern

A Black Horse Western

ROBERT HALE · LONDON

© 1973, 2005 Frederick Nolan
First hardcover edition 2005
Originally published in paperback as
Trap Angel by Frederick H. Christian

ISBN 0 7090 7642 8

Robert Hale Limited
Clerkenwell House
Clerkenwell Green
London EC1R 0HT

Typeset by
Derek Doyle & Associates, Shaw Heath.
Printed and bound in Great Britain by
Antony Rowe Limited, Wiltshire

CHAPTER ONE

The raid took exactly seventeen minutes.

The men who executed it worked with a precision that only comes from much training and complete confidence. They knew how the Fort worked as accurately as if they had seen the duty rosters. And they were completely, utterly ruthless.

Two men took each sentry in dark corners, knifing them with savage efficiency and in complete silence. Three others took out the guard room and its occupants, a sergeant and two soldiers who were having a quiet smoke before checking the perimeter for the last time before Taps. The sergeant managed to yell once before he was smashed to the ground by the barrel of a sixgun, his skull caved in from the force of the blow but the two soldiers never even got to their feet. They just had time to realise that the three men were intruders and the questioning look was

5

still in their eyes as they died beneath the hungry knives. The three raiders stood in the bloody room, their breath coming in ragged bursts and the tallest of them nodded towards the wall, where a series of key rings hung in a row on nails. They lifted the ring labelled 'Armoury' and sifted silently across the empty parade ground. The four companions were waiting for them, eyes wary for movement. The Fort McEwan Young Men's Club was holding a dance, and from the officers' mess the brass band strain of 'Yellow Rose of Texas' thumped in unison with the stamp of soldier boots on the chalked floor. Every man not physically on duty was there whirling his favourite laundress around – or a bunkie if he was out of luck with the ladies – and the little noise the raiders made hardly dented the blast of sound from in there.

The raiders brought their wagon on well-oiled wheels to the door of the Armoury. There was a heavy padlock on the door. The tall man who had killed the sergeant nodded and one of the others put a strip of iron between the arm of the lock and its body and then wrenched. There was the tensile *spang* of breaking metal and the door was open. The seven men formed a human chain passing the weapons out from the Armoury. The leader counted forty-two Springfield rifles, seventeen Army Colts and three .50 Sharps' breechloaders. After that those inside moved to

the shelves holding the cardboard boxes of
ammunition. They had shifted about two thousand rounds when the leader gave a signal and
they halted, sifting outside in the darkness.

The bright light across the parade ground
limned their position but made the shadows in
which they worked even deeper. They could see
people on the porch of the officers' quarters.
Some of them were drinking from punch cups.
Once in a while the lighter ripple of a woman's
laughter could be heard above the basso rumble
of the male voices.

'The gate,' the leader said.

One of his men got aboard the wagon and
moved across towards the gate. There were half a
dozen tame Apache playing mumbletypeg at the
foot of the gatepost, and they looked up dully as
the wagon came to a halt and the two guards
walked idly across to check it. One of them was
humming a waltz the band was playing inside.
The man on the wagon said something to the first
guard, who grinned and lifted the tarpaulin on
the wagon bed. He reeled back as the man
beneath the tarp planted a foot of Bowie knife
into his throat. The second guard shouted something, whirling to get his rifle which was leaning
against the stairs going up to the lookout. As he
turned one of the raiders hit him with the barrel
of a sixgun and the young soldier slid sideways
into the dirt, one hand clawing for a moment in

7

the dust before he went rigid and then finally limp. The Indians scattered as the wagon was whipped to a gallop, the horses lunging against the traces as the phalanx moved out fast into the night-shrouded plain. One of the Indians ran towards the parade ground shouting the alarm and out of the night came the flat hard sound of a carbine being fired. The Apache went cartwheeling forward, plunging into the dirt at the feet of the young officer who had come running down the steps from the big wooden building where the dance was going on. The young officer was very good, and did all the right things. He rapped out orders, sending men scurrying, bugles sounded across the empty Fort and lights sprang up in the enlisted men's barracks.

But by the time the patrol was mounted and set in pursuit there was no sign of the raiders at all.

CHAPTER TWO

The Attorney-General smacked his palm flat on
the desk.

'Angus,' he said, 'we're in trouble.'

Angus Wells, sitting in the chair opposite the
Attorney-General's desk, said nothing. He was a
man who didn't talk any more than he had to. He
liked that 'we' though. When you were in trouble
with the Old Man, *you* were in trouble right up to
your hairline. When he was getting a hard time
from above, however, it was 'we' who were in trouble. That old joke: we share the work – he leaves
it, and I do it.

'Trouble,' the Attorney-General repeated. He
tossed some papers across the desk, his lip curling
with distaste.

'You've read these?'

Wells nodded. The report of the Officer of the
Day at Fort McEwen. The findings of a Court of
Inquiry to investigate the robbery of the Armoury
there – both useless, since the men who had seen

9

the raiders had all been killed and everything else merely confirmed what any fool could see.

'What do you make of them?' The Attorney-General asked.

'Not a lot,' Wells replied. 'The most valuable thing in them is the list of what was stolen.'

'Sixty-two guns,' fumed the man behind the desk 'Eighteen hundred rounds of ammunition.'

'Eighteen hundred and sixty-five,' Wells corrected him.

'God damn it, eighteen hundred and sixty-five, then,' said the Attorney-General testily. 'Stolen off a United States Army installation while they were holding a dance. A dance!'

He savoured the word, as if in holding it the soldiers had been guilty of committing acts of gross indecency in the middle of Pennsylvania Avenue.

'What's your interest in this, anyway?' Wells asked. 'Can't the Army do its own investigation?

'Aye, they can. And they will, or Phil Sheridan is going to have somebody's guts for a watchfob. But that's not all, you see.'

Wells sat up in his chair. 'What else?' he said quietly.

'I had a hunch,' the Attorney-General said. 'Got Phil Sheridan to look into the records for me. There was a similar raid at Fort Stanton in New Mexico Territory two months ago. Nobody at the Army had connected them.'

'And. . . ?'

'That time they got fifty-seven revolvers and twenty-four brand new Winchester repeaters, not to mention fifteen hundred rounds of ammunition.'

Wells did some rapid sums and didn't like the answer.

'That's a hell of an arsenal someone's putting together,' he said.

'I know it,' came the reply. 'And I want to know who. And why. Somebody out there is planning to raise merry hell, or I'm a Dutchman. Somebody who knows everything he needs to know about the Forts he raids and what's in their armouries. Someone who has killed a dozen men or more getting what he wants. The President talked about putting that charlatan Allan Pinkerton on the case, but I talked him out of it. Says he wants it all cleared up before July. Going out there for some political convention, and doesn't want any awkward questions thrown at him, he says. Political necessity, those were the words he used. Political necessity.'

Wells didn't rise to that one. The office of Attorney-General was a Presidential appointment and even if the present incumbent didn't have much truck for his peers, he was just as much a politician as any of them.

'These reports all we have?' he asked.

'That and the garbled descriptions given by

some Indians who saw the raiders at McEwen,' the older man said. 'You'll get them all from Records, for what they're worth which isn't much.' He paused, then looked at Wells shrewdly. 'Any ideas?'

'Not that I can think of,' Wells admitted. 'I'll get on to it.'

'You'll put someone on it?'

Wells looked up, allowing his surprise to show.

'I figured you wanted me to handle it myself,' he said.

The Attorney-General started to speak, hesitated, and then busied himself lighting one of his long black cigars. His head wreathed in pungent smoke, he shifted uncomfortably in his leather-backed chair.

'It's – they – hell and damnation, Angus!' he burst out, 'What I'm trying to say is I don't know whether I ought to let you go in your condition.'

'That's a hell of a thing for you to say to me,' Wells said.

'Dammit, Angus, now don't you go getting sulky on me,' the Attorney-General said angrily. 'You got yourself shot to pieces down Lordsburg and I—'

'Just wondered if I could cut the mustard,' Wells said quietly. 'Havin' only one hand and one good leg, like.'

'You could send someone else,' the older man said. 'That new youngster, what's his name—?'

'Angel,' Wells said. 'He's not ready yet.'

'One of the others, then,' the Attorney-General said. 'Maybe—'

'Sir.'

Wells' voice was flat and unemphatic. The man behind the desk stopped in mid-sentence and frowned. But he listened.

'Every doctor in the District of Columbia has said I'm fit,' Wells said. 'I can ride as well as I ever could. I've learned to use my left hand as well as I ever used my right. They didn't shoot me in the head. So what's your objection to my going?'

'Ahhhh.' The Attorney-General waved his cigar. 'I just thought . . .'

'With respect, sir,' Wells went on relentlessly. 'You know we're short staffed. You know this can't wait. And you know I can handle it.'

'All right, all right,' came the testy answer. 'You've made your point. Go get your fool head shot off again.'

Wells grinned, his face becoming boyish. 'Not hardly,' he said.

'Good. That's all settled then,' said the Attorney-General. 'Will you need any help?'

'If I do I'll send for it.'

'Where will you begin?'

'Fort Stanton is the nearest, I'll start there. I can be in Trinidad by Friday, and out at Stanton before the weekend's over. I know some people out there. From last time.'

'That youngster Angel knows that country, doesn't he?'

Wells nodded.

'Why don't you take him along, Angus?'

Wells didn't let his grin show this time. He knew what the Old Man was up to. But he also knew that he himself needed to go this one alone, perhaps to prove to himself that he was all the things he had just convinced his chief that he was: fit, and capable, and able to carry on as before in a very tough job, twisted leg and useless hand notwithstanding.

'He's in training, and I don't want to interrupt that,' was all he said.

'Doing well?'

'I think so,' Wells replied, knowing the Attorney-General got a daily report on Frank Angel's progress from his instructors at what the men who worked for the Justice Department unsmilingly called 'the College'.

'Don't go taking any fool chance, Angus,' the Attorney-General said, finally. 'These men, whoever they are, are up to something that makes killing a sideline. Stealing guns from the Army is a hanging offence anywhere in the United States and they know it. They aren't going to let themselves be taken easily.'

'Show me anyone we've ever taken who was,' Wells reminded him.

'Let me know how you get on,' the Attorney-

General said gruffly. 'And send Miss Rowe in here on your way out.'

Wells got up. The Attorney-General watched him without speaking as he put his weight on the thick cane he always used and walked across to the door. Wells made a very big thing out of not fumbling over the door handles and the man behind him let a smile touch the austere mouth. They didn't come any better than his Chief Investigator but he'd be damned uphill and down dale before he'd say it out loud.

In the antechamber outside the big high-ceilinged office, Wells stopped at the desk of a tall honey-haired girl with a stunning smile. Amabel Rowe was the Attorney-General's personal private secretary and there wasn't a healthy male in the big, echoing building on Pennsylvania Avenue who had not at one time or another tried to invite her out for dinner, or the theatre, a carriage ride or a picnic. So far, no one had succeeded and there were those who referred to her as 'the Fair Miss Hard to Get'.

'The Old Man wants to see you,' Wells told her.

'Don't you let him hear you calling him that,' she said. 'Or he'll have you back shuffling papers in the basement.'

'Not sure I wouldn't prefer it,' Wells grinned. 'Nice quiet life.'

Miss Rowe got up from behind her desk and went towards the doors which led into the

Attorney-General's office. She looked back as she went in. Wells was hobbling down the corridor like a man in a hurry to get somewhere. He didn't look anything like a man who'd prefer to be shuffling papers.

CHAPTER THREE

'Again,' said the Armourer.

He placed the gun on the concrete floor. It was one of the new Colt .45 Frontier models. He pulled two cotton bales in front of it then paced out seven steps.

'Ready?' he said. Frank Angel nodded.

The Armourer went to the bank of levers at the side of the big counter which ran across the end of the range in the basement of the Justice Department building.

'Go,' he said quietly.

Angel ran forward, diving headfirst over the two cotton bales and landing on his right shoulder, head tucked down as he rolled forward picking up the gun in one smooth sweeping movement as he came up, and as he did the Armourer jerked one of the levers. A target shaped like a crouched man popped up in the lighted section at the end of the range about thirty feet from Angel, who had come to rest kneeling with the

17

hammer of the gun eared back. He fired and then fired again, rolling forward as he did to the bale of cotton placed about two yards to the right of where the gun had been laid. Again the Armourer jerked the lever and again the figure jerked upright. Angel fired twice more. The sounds of the shots slammed against the white-painted walls. He stood up, punching the used shells from the chamber as the Armourer turned a wheel which brought the target along sagging wire towards the counter. He lifted it from its metal holders and looked at it with pursed lips.

'Not bad,' he said grudgingly and handed it to Angel.

There were four holes in the target. Two were placed high on the shoulder of the cutout figure, while the other two had perforated it just above what would have been the line of the belt the man might have been wearing.

'He could still be on his feet,' the Armourer remarked.

'Maybe,' Angel grinned.

'You wouldn't want to find out the hard way,' the Armourer said without any humour in his voice at all. 'Let's try it again.'

He reloaded the gun and they started over.

Frank Angel stretched out on the bed in his apartment on F Street. Every muscle in his body throbbed from the constant physical action. He felt the tug of fatigue from reflexes dulled by the unceasing demands upon them. He had been working with the Armourer for four days now, yet still the man professed himself dissatisfied, never once offered a word of encouragement. If – as had once happened – Angel suggested that shooting at a target under whatever difficulties the Armourer could dream up, was hardly comparable to shooting at a man who could shoot back and kill you, the only reaction he got was a grunt. And perhaps later some fiendish little test: four different revolvers stripped down and all the parts mixed up – *All right, Angel, put 'em together. You got just ten minutes.*

The training programme, as Wells had warned him when they first came to Washington, was rigorous and exhaustive and merely average performance was not tolerated.

He went back over the last few months, recalling his disappointment when they came out of Union Station into the muddy thoroughfare of the capital city. The place was a clamour of building, everything either half erected or half torn down. The grandiose monument to Washington that had never been completed sat like a broken factory chimney on the Mall, pigs scavenging at its base. The President's home, 'the White House', still had no toilets, Angel learned. He guessed you could figure out what L'Enfant had had in mind if you sat down and worked at it. Nobody would ever make him understand why they had decided to build the capital of the United States smack in the middle of a swamp.

The Department had given him little time for sightseeing.

Within two weeks, he was in New York, warily watching the fringes of the underworld with astonishment: Bowery boys and Dead Rabbits parading in their street gang finery and ready to cut the throat of any man for the price of a drink. At City Hall they filled him in on political fixing and corruption, on the ways and means of Tammany, on the social and sexual forces brought to bear by unscrupulous men on the make – all 'good for the education' they told him, and a necessary addition to the massive readings of Blackstone's Commentaries, of Federal and Territorial laws, military and civil laws, laws governing Indian administration and land laws – Desert land and Homestead land and Indian land and pre-empeted land, land in the public domain and Spanish grant land, water rights, rights of earlier occupation, criminal jurisprudence and contract law – leaving him alone for hours and hours in lofty echoing chambers lined with heavy leather bound books, reading until his eyes went sandy and grainy and he could not remember anything.

Then the practical work. Basic survival. Tracking. How to stay alive in the desert, in the mountains, stranded alone in any wilderness. Disguises: how to alter the appearance by makeshift means, a smudge of boot blacking beneath the eyes, adding a limp to one's walk, the wearing of eyeglasses, combing the hair differently, adopting a slight accent. Navigation by the sun, by the stars. And weapons, always more and more about weapons. Knives, guns, rifles, spears, bows, arrows, swords, clubs, staves, hatchets, explosives – their values, their uses, their limitations. Culminating in the tests: they took him on a train and then on horseback somewhere hours away from the city and turned him loose in a swampy wilderness without food, water or weapons. They gave him a one-hour start and then sent three trained men after him. He had to elude them and get back to a house in a clearing somewhere in the swamp. It took him four days and he lost eighteen pounds doing it, but he made it. En route he had learned how to find water when none seemed to exist, how to trap small wild things and subsist on their meagre, strong tasting flesh. He had learned how to conceal his lair like any hunted thing, how to defend himself in any situation. How to stay alive.

He went across the room and opened the window. The noise from the street drifted in. Somewhere he could hear a man selling newspapers and the smell of cooking food came to his nostrils. He felt hungry. Maybe he would go out and get a meal.

'You're stupid!' the instructor at 'the College' had shouted.

'Yes sir.'

'Say it!'

'I'm stupid, sir.'

'You're an insolent fool, Angel.'

'That's correct, sir.'

'You wouldn't know how to use that gun if your life depended on it.'

'If you say so, sir.'

'Damn you, Angel, don't answer me back!'

The unexpected searing shock of the slap across his face, and his own reflex action as the anger bit into his mind. He had stood there with the sixgun in his hand and the instructor had laughed.

'Look at you,' he had jeered. 'You going to shoot me, Angel?'

'I see,' Angel said softly and slipped the gun back into its holster.

'Good boy,' the instructor said as if he were a dog.

'Suppose I'd pulled the trigger,' Angel said to him afterwards. The instructor had grinned like a cat with a fat mouse.

'You don't think I'd give you a loaded gun to play with, do you?'

Angel had grinned as well. They were training him. Training him to kill if he had to, but not because someone had jockeyed him into a spot where emotion dictated the action and not reason. Let no man chose the killing ground, they told him. You select it. You decide what to do. And you will stay alive.

He remembered the short squat man with the dark skin who had been waiting for him in the gymnasium one day. He never learned the man's name. They were alone and the floor was covered with the mattresses as always. The man held out a thick stick, about two feet long.

'No guns today,' he had said. 'This time it's knives.'

'Where's mine?' Angel asked.

'Here,' said the man and came at him with a wicked Bowie flat on his palm, hard and fast and without any kind of warning, a slicing cut that could have disembowelled a horse. Angel acted blindly, instinctively, smashing down on the man's wrist with the heavy stick. The man grinned and fell back and Angel saw he had heavy leather bands strapped around his wrists. Then he came back in again, shifting the knife very fast to his left hand and lifting the blade towards Angel's ribcage. Angel moved fast on his feet and brought the stick around and as he turned jerked backwards with it and the blunt end hit the man with the knife beneath the breastbone, bringing breath whooshing out of him with a great gust. He went down on one knee as Angel whirled around with the stave cocked in both hands, but the man rolled away before he could deliver a blow and came up smoothly on his feet as if without effort, eyes hooded, circling, circling, moving all the time.

'Not bad,' he said. There was an ounce of respect in his voice but no more than that.

They kept at it for almost twenty minutes. By the time they were finished both men were drenched with sweat. Angel never managed to get the knife away from his opponent, but neither did the man get another chance at Angel's body with the knife. Finally the man called a halt. His shoulders were heaving from the exertion.

'What's your name, kid?' he asked.

'Angel,' the young man replied. 'Frank Angel.'

The man nodded. 'You'll do,' he said, and pulling on a heavy woollen sweater went out of the gymnasium. Angel never saw him again and when he asked Wells about him, all Wells would say was that the man was known as 'the Indian' and was reputed to be the best knife fighter in the United States.

Angel thought about coffee. He wondered whether Mrs Rissick, his landlady, would make him some and send it up. He could use a cup of coffee. Before he went to bed he would have to bone up on Blackstone again. There was another written examination tomorrow.

Another day at the gymnasium, the instructor

had just patted him on the shoulder as he went through the door and then stepped back. It was enough to make Angel wary: by now he knew that the surprises were always sprung on you without warning. He went into the room expecting anything and was tense and ready, balanced on the balls of his feet. Then someone took hold of him and threw him across the gymnasium. He hit the mattresses with a thud that knocked him breathless and lay there for a moment, cursing silently. They never told you what to expect. They just tossed you in and left you to do whatever you could. There were no rules. Only survival counted. He got to his feet carefully, and saw the man coming at him. He just had time to realise it was a Chinese or Japanese. The man made a short, explosive sound, something like *Haaaii!* and then his feet came up and Angel went over backwards again, every ounce of wind driven from his lungs. The man was already coming after him again and Angel let him take hold but this time he managed to throw a feinted left jab and followed it with a very short, wicked and lethal right cross. Fast as it was, Angel saw the little man grin as he avoided the punch and then Angel went up and over and came down flat and hard on the floor. The little man smiled and stepped back. There was no humour at all in the slanting eyes which weighed Angel as if were a leg of pork. The little man bowed.

'Unarm combat,' he said. 'I show.'

And every day for the next five days he threw Angel all over the gymnasium, until Angel's arms felt like rags, and his body was one solid, throbbing mass of aching, bruised flesh. Demonstration followed practice followed demonstration until finally each day the little man, whom Angel had now discovered was Korean, would hold up one hand in the peace sign and leave without a word. Next time, they would meet in the gymnasium and Kee Lai would stand opposite Angel, bow formally, and come at him again like a tiger. Each day Angel learned a new defence, a new series of moves. They all had names, but he remembered in the heat of the combat only the action, the swift turning kick that took the man's leg from under him, the disabling chop across the carotid artery, the maiming smash of knuckle to the Adam's apple. How to fall. How to get up fast and ready. How to choke. How to blind. How to break the brittle bones of knee and shin and wrist and elbow. Once in a while he managed to actually strike Kee Lai, and the dark slanted eyes would glow briefly with something like pride, or pleasure, or both. But mostly the little man simply let Angel attack him and then demonstrated a throw, a hold, a riposte to the action which Angel knew would have killed him had it been delivered. In their second week, Kee Lai began to explain some of the things

26

Angel was learning.

'*Judo* is basic discipline,' he said. 'Now you learn *karate*.'

'What's that?'

'Most dangerous,' was the succinct reply.

Angel groaned and the little Korean grinned.

'When you get to highest level of *karate* then you will learn *aikido*,' he said.

'Don't tell me,' Angel said. 'That's even more dangerous, right?'

The Korean nodded. 'In my country man who know *aikido* never fight anyone. Never.'

'Your county is in China, isn't it?'

Kee Lai nodded, his swarthy face grim.

'Very bad place my country.' He would say no more about it.

Now he taught Angel the breathing exercises, and the internal disciplines that go with the learning of *karate*. Because perhaps he sensed Angel's genuine interest, he told him about the great Chinese historians and philosophers, Sun Tzu, Wu Ch'i, Lao Tzu.

'To rise,' Kee Lai told him, 'a man must first fall. To grow, he must first become smaller. To take, you must give. Taking of the strength of an adversary you are given strength. You must control all of yourself here—' he gestured at his belly 'in the *tan t'ien*. There is a force, which we call *ch'i*. If you can summon it at will, you are truly stronger than ordinary man.'

27

And they went back to the mattresses and Kee Lai again threw Angel all around the room. Slowly, slowly, the younger man gained cunning and caution and knowledge. Gradually, Kee Lai found it harder to throw him at will. Eventually, he was himself thrown by Angel. And then their sessions were at an end. On the last day, the Korean held up his hand for halt, and bowed, as usual, to signal the end of their training. As Kee Lai straightened up Angel hit him with an uppercut as sweet as anything he had ever put together. The little man's eyes bugged with surprise as he went over and backwards and down, out for the count. Angel got a wet cloth and slapped the high cheekbones until the Korean's eyes flickered and he came around.

'Old American proverb,' Angel grinned. 'There's more ways of skinning a cat than one.'

Kee Lei sat up, rubbing his jawbone ruefully, something in his eyes that Angel could not define. It was the nearest he had ever seen Kee Lai to smiling, but all the little man said was 'Ha!' as he got up and went out of the gymnasium. Although he had no more sessions with the Korean, one day Wells brought in an envelope to Angel. In it, beautifully scripted on fine rice paper, was something written in Chinese. They got one of the Embassy people to translate it for them. It said 'Confucius says: what you do not want others to do to you, do not do to others. Old

28

Chinese proverb.' It was not signed.

Frank Angel got up from the chair and went down the stairs to the street. There was a hash house on the corner of Massachusetts Avenue and he ate a steak and two eggs with fried potatoes and drank about half a gallon of coffee. He wondered what Angus Wells was doing.

CHAPTER FOUR

It was a long haul from Trinidad but most of it was downhill. Lieutenant Philip Evans, 9th United States Cavalry, eased his backside into a more comfortable spot on the McClellan saddle and turned to watch the wagons moving down the snakelike trail off the Raton Pass. Ahead of them and below the country lay like the landscape in your dreams, near enough to touch but stretching so far into the distance that you knew you could never traverse it. Off into the far blue distance the dusty world unrolled, punctuated here and there by the purple upthrust of flat topped mesas darkening in the long light of evening. Away off to the south-east he thought he could see the sparkle of light touching the Canadian River. He still could not get used to the idea that he was here, in the uniform of a Lieutenant of the United States Army, commanding men in the Territory of New Mexico, guarding wagons lurching dangerously in the deep ruts of the Santa Fe Trail.

Evans felt the romance of the past strongly – and here more than most places, he felt, one could actually touch it. Across these very stones had rolled the caravans of Bent and St Vrain and Becknell and Gregg. All the panoply of history had passed this way: Philip St George Cooke and Christopher Carson, Zebulon Pike and Kearney, they and thousands of ordinary people heading for the bright land and the new future promised at the end of the trail in the city of the Holy Faith of St Francis. Even the place names had a magical, golden aura. When he wrote home to his parents in Boston, he would tell them how he had sat on his horse beside the Trail, commanding the troop that was escorting the three lumbering wagons down the curving, winding road and thought of them. He would perhaps embroider it all a little, excite their staid Eastern imaginations with his word pictures, and the exotic names of the rivers and mountains, the Purgatoire and the Canadian and the Pecos – that would get his old aunts chattering away in the ivy-covered Beacon Hill house. He breathed in a deep draught of the clear mountains air. New Mexico Territory. He had been here six weeks. Already he loved it.

'Straighten up there, soldier!' he shouted.

The wagon had drawn level with the spot where he sat on his horse but the troopers had failed to spot him and were slouching along in their saddles, letting the animals do the work, sensibly relaxing while there was an opportunity to do so. They stiffened their backs as he touched the spurs to his horse's flanks and cantered off to the head of the column.

'G.D.F.' muttered Private Frank Casey. He spat a gobbet of tobacco juice off to leeward, making his horse shy violently. 'Whoa, you bitch!'

'What's G.D.F. mean, Frank?' asked a trooper alongside him.

'God Damned Fool!' snapped the older one. 'Which is what that popinjay is. I bet he never sweated in his life.'

There was an aggrieved tone in his voice. Since Lieutenant Evans had joined the Regiment, he had given none of them any pleasure. Old Campaigners like Casey resented an officer who expected men to ride as if on parade when all they were doing was wet-nursing a couple of wagons, and to watch their tongues when the muleskinners driving the teams were doing their best to invent a day-long dialogue of curses without repeating themselves once.

'How far to the Fort?' someone asked.

'Seventy miles, give or take,' another replied.

'Shee-hit!' growled Casey. 'That's three, four more days of eating dust and smellin' muleshit.'

'Take it easy, Frank,' said Private Barber, riding alongside him. 'It sure beats haulin' wood back at the Fort.'

'I ain't so damned sure,' Casey growled. 'At least we ain't expected to be little tin sojer boys for some fancy-fuckin' dude shavetail.'

'That'll be enough of that, Casey!' snapped a deeper voice. Cantering alongside the six-man troop came its Sergeant, Eric Mackenzie. Mackenzie was short, and built as the old Army saying had it, like an adobe latrine. He had fists like knots in a hawser and a temper that very few of his troopers having experienced it ever cared to arouse. His face was scoured a sandstone brown from the years in the saddle indicated by the row of hashmarks on his uniform sleeve.

'You heard what the Lieutenant said,' he growled. 'Straighten them backs up, now. Try to look like soldiers instead of bloody pisspot vendors. An' keep those bloody idle tongues still or ye'll all end up policin' the parade ground until you've got curvature of the spine!'

'Yes, sarge!' shouted Casey, snapping upright in the saddle as the other five troopers followed suit. 'You old bastard,' he added softly, but not until Mackenzie was out of earshot. They came on down the Trail, the road more level now as they left the mountain pass. There were huge boulders on both sides of the road, and heavy timber clothed the slopes behind them. The sun slipped a few thousand miles further down the sky and off to the right they could hear wild turkeys gobbling.

It was at that moment that the raiders hit them.

They had it all carefully planned and the troopers never really had a chance. Three men on each side of the road behind sheltering boulders laid down a withering crossfire and repeating rifles that emptied three saddles before Mackenzie could yell out the order that his surviving men had already anticipated, falling out of their saddles and running for shelter, any shelter from the scything hail of seeking death. The ambushers now turned their attention to the wagons, and the troopers, fumbling with their ammunition pouches and thumbing loads into the clumsy Springfields saw first one and then two of the wagon drivers whacked off their board seats as if they had been hit with invisible clubs. One of them hit the ground in a tight bundle, his legs driving him around in a circle that pushed up hillocks of earth, slowing as the ground darkened with his blood until he kicked twice and then stretched out as if for sleep.

'Holy Mother of God!' breathed Private Casey, 'will ye look at that?'

That was Lieutenant Philip Evans. After the first stunning shock of the deadly fusillade had startled his fractious horse, Evans had spent all his energy controlling the animal. Now he wheeled around and drew the revolver from his holster, pointing the pistol dead ahead of him over his horse's ears, and jammed iron into the animal's flanks. The horse erupted into a gallop dead straight towards the rocks where the ambushers were hidden, and as he swept past where Mackenzie and the other troopers lay hugging he yelled 'Follow me, men!' and bucketed up the hill away from them.

'Up yours, Charlie!' said Casey loyally.

They watched in aweful anticipation as the young Lieutenant charged madly towards the hidden ambushers and it seemed to the soldiers that there was a moment of long empty waiting in which the universe held its breath. Then the rifles spoke in unison and they watched Lieutenant Evans cartwheel over the head of his horse. The horse slewed sideways into the rocks, a bullet through the head as Evans crashed to the ground, his pistol flying in a long slow arc through the air unfired, bright blood staining the boyish face.

'Let's get the hell out of here!' yelled Mackenzie. 'On your feet!'

The four soldiers scrambled to their feet, Springfields to port, running flat out across the broken rocky ground towards the wagons. They knew that if they could get the solid cover of the heavy wagon beds between themselves and their attackers they had a fighting chance of holding them off, but their attackers knew that too and gave none of them a chance. In the thirty yards between them and shelter they were cut down like rabbits in an open field, mercilessly and precisely. There was a long and empty silence after the sound of shooting died. Nothing moved except the busy flies, which deserted the sweating backs of the mules for the sweet smell of blood. The raiders came out from behind their rocks. Two, five, seven, ten men, led down the slope by a tall, ramrod-straight man of perhaps fifty years, his hair iron-grey and his eyes cold and without pity. As they approached the wagons, the last teamster, who had hidden beneath one of the wagons, rose to his feet, his eyes shifting from man to man, his face bathed in sweat, the stink of fear rising from him like a fog.

'In the name of God,' he wheezed. 'Don't kill me, Jesus, don't—'

He advanced towards them, hands extended pleadingly, stumbling over the stony ground. The grey-haired man made an impatient gesture and one of his men shot the teamster through the chest. The man went down flat dead. Nobody looked at him.

They went over to the wagons and quickly checked the loads beneath the tarpaulins. One of them came across to where the grey-haired man was standing tapping his beautifully shined riding boots with a leather crop. 'All in order, Colonel,' he said.

'Good,' the Colonel replied. 'Get them moving.'

'Yessir,' said the man. He yelled an order and

36

three of the men swung up into the driving seats on the wagons. Within minutes they were tooling them down the road. They swung them off on a trail that led west of the main trail and up towards Tinaja Peak. And then they were gone. Behind them nothing moved for a long, long time. A buzzard swept down from the high hills and soared above the scene of the ambush. With casual beauty, it soared on the air currents high above, circling lower towards the bloody bodies on the ground. Presently another buzzard came to join it, and then a third and more. They waited in the wide sky and still nothing moved. Then one of them swooped down and landed croaking on a rock near the body of Sergeant Mackenzie. Suddenly it flapped away, squawking in alarm as Lieutenant Philip Evans groaned aloud and tried to get to his feet. There was caked blood all over his face and for a moment he thought he was blind. He slumped back on the ground, his head spinning with nausea. After a while he managed to sit up. He saw first the body of his dead horse.

'Canteen,' he said. The thought of water was the only one in his universe and it took him the best part of ten minutes to crawl across to the horse and unhitch the canteen from the saddle. When he had drunk the canteen dry he stood up and looked around him. He saw where he was and he saw what had happened and he fell back against the burning rocks, his stomach tightening and he retched and retched again.

Then when he could stand, when he could think again, he staggered down the rocky hillside to where the men lay dead.

CHAPTER FIVE

Angus Wells had learned little in Fort Stanton and less in Fort McEwen. The Army reports had told it all and there was little more anyone could add. In addition, the military didn't take all that kindly to Government snoopers coming around telling them their business. Wells had got a very cold shoulder in some quarters. Questioning the Indians had been a complete waste of time. Far too many others had already questioned them and now they were anxious to say anything the white man seemed to want them to say, embroidered, like moccasins, to order.

So Wells bid the hard-drinking cavalrymen an unregretful farewell and headed across the Rio Grande valley and up towards Santa Fé. The United States Marshal for the Territory had his office in Santa Fé, in the Federal buildings which had been built on ground that had once been part of the old Plaza. Wells let his horse pick its way through the narrow unpaved alleys which

passed for streets in Santa Fé. The cathedral bell
was clanging: it sounded as if someone were beat-
ing on it with a stick. Dogs and mules roamed
everywhere. The place looked cheap, primitive,
and highly unsanitary. Ragged children played in
the dust. Chickens scattered before the horse. Yet
Wells knew that inside the adobes that looked like
hovels he would have found light, bright-painted
walls decorated with Indian pottery and blankets,
and interior patios with tinkling fountains
watered by the endless snows of the Sangre de
Cristos. There were families in Santa Fé older
than the United States itself, their origins going
right back to the court of Philip of Spain. These
families looked upon all Americans as a curse,
considering them neither caballeros nor
Christians. In fact the Santa Fé name for an
American was *burro* – jackass. He grinned to
himself. Right now he felt they might have something.

John Sherman was a tall bluff man with a heavy
black moustache and keen blue eyes. He wore a
black vest and pants and a soft collared white shirt
open at the neck. His boots were highly polished
and he wore no pistol that Wells could see.

Sherman stood up as Wells came into the
office. Wells introduced himself and indicated
that he would prefer to talk in private. Sherman
looked at the credentials Wells showed him with
slightly raised eyebrows and then waved to a door

on one side of the room.

'Private in there,' he said, and led the way into a smaller room that looked out on to the plaza. As he closed the door he said something to one of his Mexican deputies. By the time Wells had explained his reason for being in Santa Fé the deputy had returned with a stone jug and two glasses. The jug was beaded with cold, and Sherman poured some of its ruby contents into the glasses.

'Sangria,' he said. 'Best thing they ever invented in Spain.'

The cold drink was delicious and Wells said so. Sherman nodded. 'You sound like you've got some sort of job, Wells,' he said. 'I heard a little about those army raids. I take it they haven't come up with anything?'

'Not so you'd notice,' Wells said. 'Where did you hear about them?'

'Oh, there was some talk,' the Marshal said. 'I guess some soldier came through and talked about it.'

'Interesting,' Wells said. 'I got the impression the Army people had been trying to keep it quiet.'

'You can't keep that sort of thing quiet, man.' Sherman smiled. 'This is the State capital. The Attorney-General's office is right across the way.'

'Can you recall exactly where you heard about it?' Wells insisted. 'It could be important.'

41

'You're not suggesting. . . ?'

'I'm not suggesting anything. I just don't have a pot to piss in and I can use any sort of information.'

'Well,' Sherman said. 'Wait a minute, then.'

He got up from his chair; glass in hand, and went across to the window. He looked down at the Plaza, not really seeing the old men sitting on the stone benches around the monument to the battle of Valverde.

'It was in the hotel, I think,' he said. 'La Fonda, across the way. We were taking a drink on the porch.' He grinned. 'Local custom, taking a drink in the evening after dinner. It's where the boomers and fixers get together to wheel and deal. You want to buy something, sell something, you go to the La Fonda and take a drink on the porch after dinner.'

'Can you recall who was there?'

'Legal people, mostly,' Sherman recalled. 'There'd been some dinner. Tom Catron was there. You know him, of course.'

'I know him all right,' Wells said evenly.

'I figured you would,' Sherman said. 'Him being the Attorney-General.'

'Go on,' Wells persisted.

'Who else, now? Bill Rynerson, from Las Cruces. Got a law firm down there. Some people from the Governor's staff. Oh, yes, I remember now. That was the night Denniston was there, sounding off.'

'Denniston?'

'Colonel Denniston, he calls himself, although where he got his rank I wouldn't know. War between the States, maybe. He was making his usual speech. The President of the United States is letting the country go to the dogs. All politicians should be shot. You know the sort of thing.'

'What's his beef?'

'Search me,' Sherman shrugged. 'He claims that the Government took some land off him, I think. Hard to say. He talks a hell of a lot but he doesn't tell you anything, if you take my meaning.'

'You know his first name?'

'Never heard anyone use it. In fact, he's something of a mystery man. His men all "sir" him as if they were still in the Army. And from what I've heard, which I repeat isn't a hell of a lot, that's about the way he runs his spread.'

'Cattle?'

'Could be giraffes for all anyone around here knows,' Sherman said, his expression rueful. 'He's got a big place up at Colfax county, on the Palo Blanco. Made himself mighty popular up there. Put a seven-foot fence around it, and has hardcases patrolling the perimeter day and night. There's signs all over, so I'm told, saying trespassers will be shot on sight.'

'Interesting,' Wells said, a question in his voice.

'Thought so myself,' Sherman agreed. 'I sent a couple of deputies over there to take a look around. Denniston's men bustled them off. No way they could get in. Since no laws had been broken there wasn't anything I could do. I asked Denniston why he wouldn't let my men in, last time I saw him. Drew himself up like a puff adder and said he'd be obliged if I would mind my own business because I could be assured that was what he was doing.'

'What about his men?'

'They all look like toughs to me, but as far as I can tell none of them is wanted in New Mexico. Of course, I haven't seen them all.'

'They come to town at all?'

'Once in a while, when Denniston comes in. As if they were some sort of honour guard. But they never get into any trouble. They don't drink. No girls, nothing. Just wait in the plaza like dressmakers' dummies until the colonel tells them to get on their nags and come home. Of course,' he added, pouring the last of the sangria into the glasses, 'they got their own little hell-town not five miles away. Kiowa. I imagine they raise all the Cain they want to nearer home. But that's enough about Denniston – I don't know why I went on about him so much. Just that he's fascinating. An enigma.'

'How long has he been around?'

'Not long. A year maybe. I can check that for you.'

'I wish you would,' Wells said. 'Colonel Denniston sounds very interesting.'

'You don't think he had anything to do with—?'

'I don't think anything,' Wells said. 'Not a thing.'

'I mean,' Sherman said. 'I mean, he's a mite on the barmy side, maybe, but he keeps himself to himself. No trouble, you know what I mean? In fact, he's pretty funny, sometimes – especially when he gets going about Grant. I don't know whether he's telling the truth of not, but he tells pretty nasty stories about the President.'

'Like?'

'Oh, vague stuff. About him being an alcoholic, about the whole Cabinet being up to its knees in graft. Stuff like that.'

Wells said nothing, just sat there and looked.

Sherman shifted uncomfortably.

'Hell, Wells,' he said. 'Out here, that kind of gossip is like water in a thirsty land. No matter if it's true or not. Nobody really takes Denniston seriously.'

'Funny,' Wells said, reflectively. 'Here you have a man who hates the President of the United States enough to tell people he's an alcoholic and an embezzler, a man who has a spread in a remote place surrounded by guards and security, a man with military knowledge and experience, a man with what you yourself called hardcases working for him – and you don't take him seriously? What

45

does it take to get you to take someone seriously, Sherman – does he have to walk around with a lighted stick of dynamite in his hand?'

Sherman looked stunned, and sat down heavily in his chair. 'Wells,' he said. 'Listen. I mean, I hadn't even thought of it like that. You just don't. I mean, it's so – wild, so improbable.'

'I'll grant you that,' Wells said grimly. 'But I want you to put every man you've got on to putting a dossier together for me about this Denniston. I want a map of the Palo Blanco area, an Army survey map if you can get it. I want to talk to the two deputies you sent up there. I want to see the records of Denniston's land filing—'

'Hell,' wailed Sherman, 'they're in Mesilla, Wells.'

'I don't care if they're on the goddamned moon, Sherman,' Wells snapped. 'I want to see them and I want to see them fast. Now get me a pencil and paper, and have someone stand by to take some messages to the telegraph office. Washington can turn up this man's military record if he has one. Move, man!'

Sherman jumped, and almost ran out into the office. He started shouting commands to his office staff, and within minutes the place was a veritable hive of industry. Sherman came back and stood looking at Wells, who was scribbling furiously on the pad he had provided. He was trembling, as if he had been physically attacked,

46

and felt the sour bile of resentment rising in his gorge. Who was this, this *cripple*, to come in here and order him about? These Government people were all the same – they came out here knowing nothing about the country or the people and expecting everyone to kiss their asses on command. Well, he for one wasn't going to take any more crap. The next time – Wells looked up and his cold eyes met those of Sherman. And for the first time Sherman realised the kind of man Angus Wells was, and every foolhardy ounce of bluster went out of his body as if it had been siphoned off with a hydraulic pump.

'Now we're in business,' Well said. If he had been tired when he arrived, he showed no sign of it now. 'Sherman, you've been a great help. Why don't you let me buy you a real drink while we're waiting for the replies to these?' He waved his hand at the sheaf of messages he had printed carefully on the yellow ruled paper. Sherman let a watery smile slide on to his face.

'Why, uh, that's be right nice, Wells,' he managed.

Wells stood up. 'Call me Angus,' he said, and stumped out of the office, leading the way into the street. He scanned the Plaza, saw a board sign that read *cantina* and headed towards it at a rate of knots that had Sherman trotting to keep up with him. Indians selling beads and coloured blankets beneath the porch of the Governor's

Palace stretched out their hands to try to attract the attention of the *Yanquis,* but Wells didn't even see them. He went into the cool darkness of the *cantina* and ordered tequila. The two men went through the courtly south-western ritual with salt and lemon and salute, and let the fiery liquid warm their bellies.

'Aaaaahh,' Wells said. He sounded happy.

Outside the street was quiet in the afternoon sun. They could not see Sherman's office, nor the man who came out of it, looking first right and then left, staying in the shadow of the squat adobe building until he came to the corner. Then he was around it and going at a fast lope down the dusty alley, heading south towards the Alameda. He had some yellow papers in his hand.

CHAPTER SIX

Kiowa was no great shapes as a town.

It straggled along the Palo Blanco canyon, houses and larger buildings scattered at each side of a road that turned S-shaped like a snake between the beetling hills that rolled back to even higher hills rising to the eight-thousand-foot peak of Laughlin.

Angel rode in across the wooden bridge that spanned the noisy river rushing on down towards its confluence with Ute Creek and then onwards to the Canadian, his eyes alert but his body slouched in the saddle like a man who has come a long, hard way. As indeed, he had. It seemed like years since he had reported to the Attorney-General in the big office overlooking the muddy bustle of Pennsylvania Avenue.

News of the attack on the military wagons had reached Washington almost simultaneously with Wells' messages from Santa Fé. The scale of the latest raid had startled even the Justice

Department: not only well over a hundred brand-new Winchesters plus ammunition, but this time a disassembled Gatling gun which had been on its way to Fort Marcy.

The Justice Department could move very fast when it had to, and it moved fast now. Within two days Angel had read every report, every file, and every dossier that could be assembled on the people involved: the young Lieutenant that Wells was even now interviewing in Fort Union; on Colonel Rob Denniston, late US Army, cashiered for cowardice in the aftermath of the battle of Chickamauga; on Johnnie Atterbow, ex-US Army sergeant, who had deserted shortly after Denniston's court-martial and now ran the fenced-off enclave in the Palo Blanco mountains, and who kept Denniston's hardcase crew in line.

He had only had time to spend a few hours with the Armourer, but no trouble had been spared to get him what he needed. And now he was sifting down the straggling street of Kiowa, and he looked every inch of what he was posing as: a saddle tramp, looking for any kind of work that paid well. Unshaven, dust-coated, his clothes stained with sweat and grime, he moved down the street, noting the long looks he got from men on the sidewalks, the absence of any sign of children in the place, the packrats playing in the refuse between the tarpaper shacks. There was only one big building, a saloon with a false front and a long

sign painted in red and gold that read 'Levy's –
The Traveller's Rest'. There was a tacky-looking
store with pans and mining equipment hanging
on strings from the porch roof, and at the end of
the street he found a livery stable of sorts. It
looked as if nobody really worked at keeping it
more than nominally clean, but he turned the
horse into the dark cool interior. A man of about
forty with shifting eyes which never met Angel's
limped forward.

'Howdy,' Angel said, swinging down. 'Like to
leave the horse here. Overnight, mebbe. Feed
him and rub him down, will you?'

'Anything you say, mister—?'

Angel ignored the implicit question. 'Where
could I get a room?' he asked.

'Levy's is the only place in town. How long you
figgerin' on stayin'?'

'Levy's, you say? That's the big place back up
the street a ways?'

The hostler nodded his eyes venomous. 'Two
dollars in advance for the horse,' he spat.

Angel fished in his jeans and gave the man two
silver dollars. He lifted the Winchester out of he
saddle scabbard and unfastened his war-bag from
the cantle, walking out of the stable into the
sunlight.

The hostler limped after him. 'Hey, mister,' he
whined. 'You never told me your name.'

'That's right,' Angel said pleasantly and walked

away, feeling the man's eyes on his back the whole way up the street. Nobody seemed to be taking a direct interest in him, and yet he had the inescapable feeling that he was being watched all the same. He shrugged. What else? He pushed into the saloon.

It was just a big room. Tables and chairs at one side. The usual gaming setups: faro, chuckaluck, monte. A long bar running the length of the place on the left hand side, ornate mirrors reflecting a display of bottles that would have done credit to a New York hotel. The place was clean by the usual standards appertaining in this part of the world, and it wasn't hard to figure the reason for that. There were about twenty people in the place, and here and there between the tables women in short spangled dresses moved, laughing with the men playing cards or drinking. Nobody took an awful lot of notice of Angel as he found himself a place at the bar, but he knew his arrival had been noted. He ordered a beer and sipped it slowly, watching the faces behind him in the mirror. Once in a while he caught a covert glance. Nothing more.

He signalled the bartender for a refill.

'Have one yourself,' he invited.

'Thanks,' said the man, a florid-faced individual with strands of hair pasted on to his balding skull and a heavy walrus moustache which concealed his mouth. 'Don't mind if I do.'

He scooped the foam off the beer with a wooden spatula and lifted the tankard in salute. '*Salud*,' he said.

Angel raised his glass to return the salute.

'Passin' through?' the bartender asked.

'Sort of,' was the non-committed reply. 'Any work in these parts?'

The bartender looked uncomfortable. 'We don't get that many people up here askin',' he said.

Angel shrugged. 'If I was asking,' he said. 'who would I see?'

'Only one spread in these parts,' the bartender said. 'I ain't heard they're hiring.' Angel raised his eyebrows and the bartender went on, 'Colonel Denniston's place up on the Blanco.'

'What's he run?' Angel asked mildly. 'Cattle, horses – what?'

'You better ask his ramrod,' the bartender said, retreating down the bar to serve another customer.

Angel smiled to himself. In the mirror he could see several of the men at the tables listening with unconcealed interest to his conversation. He turned to face them and their eyes were hastily averted.

'Any of you gents care to tell me where this Denniston place is?'

His words produced a strained silence, and for a moment he thought he'd pushed it too far and fast. Then a man got up from a table at the back of the room and pushed his way through to stand in front of Angel. He was a giant. He had been sitting at a table with two of the women, hard-faced harpies whose sagging breasts all but hung out of their skinny dresses. He was dressed in heavy cord pants, a checked wool shirt, good leather boots that bore the evidence of recent polishing. His stance was erect. He was so obviously ex-Army that it was almost painful. Angel grinned to himself: they never forget how to play soldiers.

'Who the hell are you?' the man said hoarsely.

'Name's Angel, Frank Angel. And you?'

'I'm Johnnie Atterbrow. Angel, you say? That's a hell of a name for a man.'

'Before you start straining yourself thinking of a joke, I've heard them all,' Angel cut in roughly. 'All I want to know is how to get to this Denniston ranch.'

'What do you want to get there for?'

Angel sighed noisily. 'Well, you see, it's like this, Johnnie. A long time ago, when I was a bitty kid, my old lady introduced me to eating regularly. I kind of got into the habit. But to keep on doing it, I got to work now and then.' He spread his hands in an exaggerated gesture. 'You see my problem.' There was a snigger from someone behind Atterbrow, who whirled around, his eyes glaring. Whoever was responsible for the sound ducked his head fast enough to fool Atterbrow. He snorted and turned back to face Angel.

'Witty, too,' he snapped. 'Denniston ain't hirin'. We got a full crew. So you can just climb back on your pony an' head back the way you came.'

Angel smiled. 'I really do need a job,' he said.

'Tough shit,' snarled Atterbrow. 'Move on, cowboy.'

'You do Denniston's hiring?'

'You better believe it. An' like I said, we don't need no saddle bums.'

'Suppose I ask Denniston?'

'Nobody asks Denniston nothin' without going through me.' Atterbrow snarled. 'Now finish your beer an' get the hell on your way.'

'You're very noisy, Johnnie,' Angel said mildly, and hit him as hard as he could in the belly. Atterbrow's eyes bugged out of his head as the fist drove into his flabby gut. He went backwards like a runaway windmill, arms and legs flailing, smashing a table into kindling in his fall, the men who had been sitting at it ending up on the floor with him in a shouting jumble of bodes. Angel stood right where he had been standing, aware that the entire saloon was silent, awed, waiting for Johnnie Atterbrow's next move. Angel watched his hands. He hoped his gamble would pay off. He didn't want to have to kill the man.

Atterbrow got slowly to his feet, a frown knotting his heavy eyebrows. He shook his head.

'You just made the worst mistake of your life, sonny,' he rumbled.

That was what Angel had been waiting to hear. He unbuckled his gunbelt and laid it on the counter behind him.

'If I've got to fight you to get to see Denniston, I'm about ready to get started,' he said softly.

'You'll not be in any condition to see anyone when I'm through with you, bucko!' snarled Atterbrow.

'It hasn't crossed your mind I might whip you?'

'Not the once,' Atterbrow said. 'They're goin' to have to bury you in a sandbag to weigh your box down.'

'Talk, talk, talk,' Angel said. He stepped forward and cuffed Johnnie Atterbrow lightly across the face. In the background he heard the indrawn gasp of astonishment from those watching and then with an inarticulate scream of rage Johnnie Atterbrow launched himself at Angel, his huge fists flailing in killing arcs.

Wells made good time over the Glorieta.

Towards nightfall he was about a dozen miles from Las Vegas, hurrying the team along. Sherman had organised a fine pair of bays and a surrey and he was making good time, frankly glad that he didn't have to cover the mountainous ground on horseback. His old wounds ached. There was thunder in the air above the Sangre de

Cristos, rumbling like some faraway avalanche behind the clouds. Once in a while he felt the heavy smack of a raindrop hit his face. His mind kept going over the details of the ambush below Raton, trying to stretch his imagination to a point where he could see why anyone would want to steal a Gatling gun. Where before there had been the possibility that the stolen rifles and ammunition had been finally destined to Comancheros, or to be sold south of the border where there was an incessant market for guns, the hijacking of the Army wagons and the disappearance of the Gatling gun with its enormous firepower scotched that theory completely. He simply could not imagine what whoever had stolen the field piece intended to do with it. Shaking his head, Wells gigged the horses to an even faster trot. With luck he would make Fort Union by midday tomorrow. Maybe the young Lieutenant would be able to tell him something that might help.

Ahead of him loomed the lighter strip of Tecolote Creek. He slowed the horses as they approached the ford, timbered heavily on both sides low and close to the water. The horses splashed through the shallow flow, enjoying the cool sting of the snow-chilled stream, and Wells leaned over to scoop up some water in his hand. The movement saved his life.

He heard the flat *brr-aaa-ng* of the rifle and instantaneously the searing pain across the fleshy part of his right thigh. It was as if someone had touched him with red-hot steel. Without conscious thought he screamed at the horses, whacking them with the reins, startling the bays into a pounding gallop that took him through the soft earth at the other side of the creek with only two wheels touching the ground, dark heavy lumps of muddy loam flying high around him as the rifle spat at him again from the bushes off to his right. He heard the dull *vawuzz* as the bullet went by and now he had unshipped his old long-barrelled Colt Army, earing back the hammer clumsily as the surrey bounced on the baked road, letting go in the general direction of the ambusher, not caring about anything except making his attacker duck his head while he, Wells, put distance between himself and the ambush. Something whacked one of the horses. He heard the slug hit the animal, the right hand one of the pair, and it faltered, breaking stride, then picked up its stride again, the other horse and the momentum of their movement taking it along. Wells threw another shot and then another into the bushes, without much hope. The distance was far too great for accurate shooting with a revolver. Damnation! he thought. His rifle was firmly wrapped inside his bedroll in back of the surrey. Trying to get at it would require the skills of an acrobat, and he had no plans to stop and try unshipping it. Instead he concentrated on getting the best speed he could out of the horses. But the right-hand animal was faltering now, and there was bloody foam whipping backwards towards Wells from its labouring head.

No choice, he thought.

He dragged the animals to a halt, his knife already in his hand as he got down, slashing at the braces, cutting the horses apart. He reached into the back of the surrey and lifted out his bedroll, the comforting weight of the rifle reassuring as he swung on to the bare back of the horse and kicked it into a run. Once more he heard the rifle behind him speak. He hunched lower on the saddle and kept going. If he had to outrun the man, at least he had a start. That last shot had sounded as if it had come from the same stand of timber and he grinned grimly. The man was either an amateur or an optimist to think he could hit a running man on horseback from more than four hundred yards. He was just congratulating himself when the second man in the rocks forty yards ahead of him shot the horse out from between Angus Wells' knees.

CHAPTER SEVEN

In a way Angel was sorry for what he had to do to Atterbrow. But he had no real choice. The man was huge. He towered a good four inches above Angel's six feet, and outweighed the slighter man by at least forty pounds. There was no question of fighting what was laughingly called man-to-man. Atterbrow would gouge and kick and maim if he could bring his superior height and weight to bear. If those hamlike fists ever connected, Angel knew they would break whatever bone they hit.

So when Atterbrow came at him, Angel simply swayed, summoning all of himself to that place, concentrating on his own *ch'i*, just as Kee Lai had taught him. Atterbrow's rocklike fist went *whap!* past his left ear as Angel let the man's brute rush take him across Angel's body, turning his own shoulder to the right and down and then driving backwards with all his force added to the speed of the bigger man, his elbow cocked and rigid, driving like a ramrod into the unprotected ribs of Johnnie Atterbrow, who went smashing into the bar face first, roaring with rage and the pain of at least two ribs cracked.

'Aaaaaaaaaaahhh!' he shouted.

It was not the pain, although the pain was in it. It was the insane fighting raging roar of an outraged bull, and if there had ever been any science or skill inside Atterbrow's brain it was driven out now by the searing white burn of total madness, the madness of frustration and shame and rage at this slim, unconcerned man with the cold eyes standing unmarked before him.

He came forward without warning, very fast on his feet for a man so big, the meaty hands spread and reaching for some kind of grip on Angel. Angel let him come and when Atterbrow got properly hold of him and started to pull Angel came forward all at once and with every ounce of strength he had, his hand coming up cocked backwards, the heel coming up beneath Atterbrow's unprotected jaw with smashing force, jarring the bear head back, bone going somewhere, mashing the cursing lips and driving Atterbrow backwards and down to the floor. Spitting out broken pieces of yellow teeth, blood spraying from his torn lips, Atterbrow came off the floor in a long diving movement, aiming for Angel's middle, every ounce of his weight behind the manoeuvre which, had it been effective, would have whirled Angel off his feet and into a wrestler's mauling tangle, where Atterbrow would have all the advantage. It was a good move. It really should have done exactly what Atterbrow – and every one of those watching – expected it would do. But it did not. Angel moved even faster than his opponent had and his two hands looped together and came down in much the same movements that they would have done if he had had an axe in his hand chopping wood. They hit Atterbrow behind the ear with a dull meaty thwack that sounded like a butcher taking a cleaver to a side of beef and drove him face down to the board floor, smashing him flat in the bloody sawdust. Again Angel stepped back, untouched. A bystander gaped at him as if he were supernatural, then switched his attention back to Atterbrow, who was again getting to his feet, his whole face a torn and awful smear of broken flesh and bone. He got to his feet, staggering, reaching again for his elusive opponent. Angel shook his head and hit him again.

His hand hardly seemed to move, and yet there was all the driving force he could muster behind the ramrod movement that drove his clenched fist, middle knuckles protruding in the karate fighting style, into Atterbrow's breast just below the heart.

The man stopped, paralysed, his eyes bulging, face purpling as his astonished system tried to carry on pumping oxygen through to the heart literally stunned by the terrible force of the blow. Still the brain commanded the arms, and again Atterbrow reached for Angel, his lips gaping like a newly-landed fish. Breath wheezed into his labouring throat. He staggered. Then he lurched forward, and Angel let him come, taking the man's grip on his left arm, turning his own hand to clamp Atterbrow's right, pulling until Atterbrow came forward on his toes. Then Angel hit the man across the forearm with his clenched fist. Everybody in the room heard the terrible sound of the bone going. It sounded like when a kid breaks a dead branch off a tree. Atterbrow made no sound, so deep in shock and pain was he. He went down to his knees again, slumped in the centre of the bloody circle of astonished watchers, his left arm useless at his side. Somewhere in his brain, something tried to make the wrecked thing get to his feet.

'Hel,' the thing said. 'Mu.'

Nobody moved. All eyes turned to see what Angel would do. No man had ever stood up to Johnnie Atterbrow before. This one didn't even look out of breath and yet he had broken Atterbrow, broken the man the way an idler on a porch snaps a match. They regarded Angel with

63

almost superstitious awe.

'Help him!' Angel snapped. 'He's probably got more guts than all of you put together. Get him on a table. Bartender! Bring a cloth and some water. Somebody get a doctor if there is one in this dump!'

'I'll go, mister,' one of the girls said, and ran for the door in a flicker of tarnished sequins and white, plump thighs. The bartender came around the bar, anxious now to help. Everyone was suddenly anxious to assist. They would probably have tried to fly if Angel had told them to do it; anything rather then see that cold killing light rekindle in the relentless eyes.

'Mister,' wheezed the bartender. 'I never seed anything like that in all my days. Never once. What kind of fighting was that, anyway?' He patted at Atterbrow's broken face with the cloth, wiping away the smeared blood, tutting as he worked.

When Angel made no answer, he went on, 'Not that it matters. Your life ain't worth a plugged nickel when the Colonel hears about this. If I was you I'd get the hell out of Kiowa before he does. Or he'll kill you sure.'

'That'll be the day,' Angel said.

'Indeed it will, sir,' said a cold voice touched with venom behind him. He heard the metallic triple click of a revolver being cocked and froze, his eyes darting to the bar where his gun lay still in its holster. No chance. He let his shoulders relax.

'Turn around, mister,' the voice said. 'I'd like to see what you look like before I kill you.'

CHAPTER EIGHT

They had him and Wells knew it.

All night he had lain hidden in the rocks alongside the trail where he had scrambled as the horse died beneath him. He had managed to get his war-bag and his rifle during the night, and had shifted around until he had a little centre point of rocks which could only be approached across open ground. He had hoped they might try to come after him during the night; there would have been a chance if they had. But he realised now that his ambushers were not amateurs as he had first supposed. The first man had been placed specifically to drive him into the sights of the second and now they were waiting for sunup to finish the job. He had no way of knowing how many more of them there were, or where they were hidden. But he had spent some time wondering who they might be and why they had laid for him at all. They could of course be common footpads, waylaying men travelling alone, but thieves would not set up so elaborate a whipsawing. Which meant that they were after him specifically. That, in turn, had to mean that his investigation had bothered someone enough to have them send men after him. And that in turn meant his hunch had been correct. There was something fishy about this Colonel Denniston. He grinned mirthlessly. Much damned good the knowledge was going to do him.

The sky was lightening rapidly now and the long low rays of the dawning sun were diluting the purple of the shadows at the base of the hills to the west. It would be full light in a very short while. The morning warmth was welcome, and he eased his cold, cramped legs. He could have done with some coffee.

Wells moved very carefully forward and poked his hat around the rocks on the end of his carbine barrel. Almost immediately a rifle spoke up in the rocks, smacking splinters off the boulder and whining away into infinity. Wells pulled back, chilled by the ambusher's proximity. That shot had come from no more than fifty yards away. He tried to remember the lie of the land, but his impression of it was vague. The trail snaked ahead, he knew, to a bend that had run between two heavy stands of pine skirting the road. The land rose to the right of the road in a sharp incline, boulders and chunks of rock scattered on

it, detritus from some prehistorical earth movement. On the left hand side of the road, the land
sloped on down into a coulee. Probably a wash,
he thought, a little stream running into Tecolote
Creek. And probably fifty yards from where he
was across ground without any form of shelter
except stunted sage and prickly pear. No way, he
told himself. Even if you could run, which you
can't. Not for the first time Wells damned the
man who had crippled him, hoping that whatever
hell Cravetts was in it was good and hot. No
escape that way. But he had to move soon. Those
bushwhackers weren't going to wait much longer.

As if in direct response to his thought, another
carbine whanged a shot at his position. The bullet
caromed off the rock face to one side, and fell
spent against the side of another. Then the
second rifle opened up, but this time the man
shooting it kept on levering and firing in one
long continuous roll, *whang-whang-whang-whant-
whang*, his slugs moving across the redoubt where
Wells had flattened himself to the ground, the
ricochets screaming, flickering blurs of stone and
flint stinging the hiding man's exposed body.

He had to move, and he knew they were doing
this to make him, which meant he couldn't move.
Yet if he stayed put, those seeking, ricocheting
bullets would eventually find the correct place,
the perfect angle – and turn inwards into him. He
shuddered at the thought of being hit by one of

those deformed, tumbling bullets. They would tear a man open like a fighting bull with a broken horn.

He rolled over on his back and sat up, levering his own Winchester and throwing a curving arc of four shots at the places where he figured the shots had come from. If he hit anything there was no sign of it. Then he got down again quickly as the second rifleman again whacked two shots at him. The sun was climbing high now. The stink of cordite clung to the tiny space in which Wells crouched. But he felt about one thin shade better than before. He thought now he knew where his ambushers were – give or take a few yards. One was up on the side of the shaly slope, about fifty yards or so straight ahead. The other was on the left hand side of the road, about twenty or thirty yards back, down below the crest of the falling ground and out of Wells' shooting line. Knowing where they were didn't improve his chances, though. If he ran up for the crest on his right, using the rocks for cover, he would be fully exposed to the ambusher in the rocks ahead of him, and as soon as he moved, the other man could run in a long half-circle and come out on the rimrod above. So Wells did the only thing he could do. He got out of his hiding place, keeping the biggest rock between him and the man in the rocks. And then he ran full tilt, the best way he could, weaving and dodging, straight at the man hidden below the crest of the falling ground on the left hand side of the trail, working the action of his Winchester fast and laying down a hail of bullets which he hoped would keep the man's head down.

It worked like a dream for the first ten yards because the big rocks behind him effectively screened him from the man on the slope and his hail of bullets whacking into the man in front of him. But in the eleventh yard Wells' form came clear of the protecting boulder and the man on the hillside calmly shot him in the back.

Wells went on forward, carried by his own momentum and that of the bullet that slewed him sideways and over the crest at the side of the trail, tumbling and rolling over and down and crashing through the thickened sage and prickly pear, the rifle flying out of his nerveless fingers.

The man on the roadside yelled in triumph and jumped to his feet, pumping wild shots at the bundling, rolling figure in its scurry of dust, but that was a mistake because Wells was not now falling, but deliberately rolling, keeping moving and ignoring the blinding pain that felt as if someone had poured molten iron into his upper body, his only instinct now to stay alive, all the years of wariness and training telling him to go on moving when every nerve in his body screamed at his brain to stay still. Wells came to a stop, pawing the old Army Colt up as the man ran towards him, throwing a shot through the dusty haze his scrambling fall had made, grunting with satisfaction as the man yelled and fell to one side, his Winchester going off as it hit the ground. Wells got to his knees, and then rolled again down and forward trying now for the coulee not fifteen yards in front of him, everything else going out of his mind except the animal need to find cover.

The man on the hillside had started running down towards the trail as he saw Wells go forward and over the first time, and he had quartered across the ground so that he was level with Wells' position and perhaps thirty yards away as Wells made his second try for safety. He went down on one knee and levelled the carbine, beading the floundering figure of the thrashing Justice Department man. He took his time and squeezed off the shot and saw Wells hesitate in mid-movement, knowing he had hit Wells again. The last desperate lunge had carried Wells to the brink of the coulee and he went off the edge, going down to the stony creek bed with his hands spread like some broken bird. The man ran up to the edge of the wash and looked down. Wells lay there broken and unmoving, his body splashed with bright blood. The man grinned, the wicked smile of a coyote that sees a calf pulled down, and levered another shell into the breech to deliver the *coup de grace*, but at that moment his companion yelled something and he hesitated. He looked

for a long moment at Wells' still form as if decid-
ing something, then ran towards his friend, who
was on his feet, curing and trying to stem the
pumping flow of blood from the bullet hole in his
upper thigh.

'Goddammit, Reed, get over here, will you?' he
shouted.

Reed ran towards his companion and laid
down the Winchester, ripping off a strip of the
man's shirt and fashioning a makeshift tourni-
quet. When the bleeding was staunched, he
slapped his friend on the shoulder.

'There you go, Mike,' he grinned. 'You'll live.'

'Goddammit, Reed,' the one called Mike
ground out, 'I thought you got him sure the first
time.'

Reed gestured at the wound on Mike's thigh.
'Shows how wrong you was,' he said flatly. 'But no
sweat. He's dead now all right.'

'Where is he?' Mike asked.

'Down in the creek bed,' Reed replied. 'I better
go make sure.'

'Shit, Reed, you hit him twice, didn't you?'
Mike grimaced. 'Even if he ain't dead, he's gonna
bleed to death down there. Ain't nobody gonna
come find him. Let's get the hell out of this: I got
to get to a doctor.'

He put his weight on the wounded leg and
swore.

'Go get the goddammed horses, will ya?' he

said. 'I'll take a look at our friend, if you like.'

'Naw, you're right Mike,' the other one said. 'He's done for. Let's get out of here. We don't want no one coming up the trail and finding us here'

They climbed laboriously back up the slope, Reed supporting his wounded comrade as best he could until they got to the stand of trees where they had left their horses. Within three minutes they were out of sight around the bend in the road that led towards Las Vegas. Behind them nothing moved except a buzzard, high in the sky, wheeling and swooping in search of dead flesh. After a while it came lower.

CHAPTER NINE

Angel looked down the bore of the Navy Colt and showed his teeth in a feral grin.

'Pull that trigger and I'll kill you,' he promised flatly, lifting his eyes to meet the equally hard gaze of the man with the gun. It had to be Denniston. Iron-grey cropped hair, eyes to match, an aquiline nose flanked by deep furrows making an arch to the thin, patrician lips. A thin-boned, aristocrat's face: or the face of a fanatic.

Denniston was dressed in a dark coat and pants which somehow had a strong military flavour, as though they might have been cut and sewn by the army tailor. The dark trousers were tucked into the tops of fine leather boots which even with their patina of dust glowed with the rich sheen of many polishings.

Denniston hesitated.

'You believe that, don't you?'

'I know it,' Angel said.

'For a man inches from death you're very sure

of yourself, Mister—?'

'Angel's the name. Frank Angel.'

'Perhaps that explains your confidence,' murmured Denniston. 'It seems a shame not to test it.'

'It would be a waste,' Angel said. 'Of both of us.'

Denniston thought about that one for a moment, and then smiled.

'I admire your nerve, Angel,' he said, lowering the gun. 'It's uncommon.'

Angel let his own tension go a little. He felt everyone in the room do the same. Denniston's men, ranged in a half circle behind their leader, looked puzzled. But Denniston ignored them. Shoving the revolver into a closed-topped holster on his belt, he went across to where Atterbrow lay unconscious. He touched the broken face lightly and then looked at Angel again, his eyes narrowing.

'What was it?' he asked. '*Karate*?'

'*Aikido*.'

'*Aikido*,' mused Denniston. 'You are indeed an uncommon saddle-tramp, Mr Angel. Suspiciously uncommon.'

Before Angel could reply to that, a little man bustled into the room, thrusting Denniston's men aside with unceremonious scorn. He went straight to where Atterbrow lay and opened the leather bag he was carrying, ignoring everyone else. Fishing a stethoscope out, he listened to the man's heart, and then grunted.

'Get him across to my office,' he said to nobody in particular. Two men came forward and lifted the unconscious form, panting under the weight as the old man turned to face Denniston, his eyes full of malice.

'Who took your man apart, Colonel?' There was scornful emphasis on the last word that brought two spots of bright colour to Denniston's cheeks. But the iron control was rigid.

'. . . *Doctor*,' Denniston said drily. 'How nice to see you sober.'

'You better pray I am if you expect that one to fork a horse this side of Christmas,' the old man retorted unabashed. 'He's been worked over better than anyone I ever saw.' Without another word he bustled out after the men carrying Atterbrow's supine form.

Denniston turned to Angel, who grinned unrepentantly. 'Well,' he said. 'Do I get the job?

'Job?'

'I asked Atterbrow if you had any work. He said I had to talk to him first. I just got through doing that.'

'I see,' Denniston said. Angel let him think about it, saying nothing. There was a long silence in the room. Someone shuffled his feet. Another coughed nervously. Then Denniston nodded.

'Let's take drink on it,' he said. 'Levy, give everyone a drink.'

And then the tension was gone completely. Men crowded to the bar, and talked to Angel, asking him questions about the fighting technique he had used. Denniston watched him as he tried to avoid the pawing that people always give the man who had come through a dangerous situation. His own men drank in a tight group at the other end of the bar. They eyed Angel with surly resentment, and Denniston grinned. *Mister* Angel might have a tougher row to hoe than he expected. The next time he had trouble Angel would find that it was gun trouble. And there wasn't a man in the Denniston enclave who wasn't very, very good.

Three hours later they were on the high divide looking down the scoured canyon on the Palo Blanco. Far behind them and below the town looked like a dirty set of building blocks left scattered by a thoughtless child. Around them tumbled the lower reaches of the mountains that went off in rising masses to Laughlin Peak and Tinaja beyond it. Off on the far side, the mountains went rolling back and upwards towards the Sierra Grande. It was a vast and lonely place, and the ten-man cavalcade looked like a column of ants in its emptiness.

Denniston and Angel rode at the head of the column and Angel asked the leader a question.

'Why here? Because of the land, man. Here

one is truly close to the grandeurs of Nature. Man's efforts seem pygmy-like compared to them. That's a healthy thing for any man to have around him. And of course,' he added with a sly grin, 'I need isolation. I want it. I cannot succeed without it.'

'Succeed at what?'

'All in good time, Mr Angel,' was the uncommunicative reply. 'All in good time. Ah, there it is!'

Angel looked down the scarred valley falling away from them. The Palo Blanco canyon was cut deep into the soft stone, its sides high and steep and treacherous on both sides of the pebble-strewn watercourse. Ahead of them the river bed turned back almost on itself, making a finger-like promontory across from which stretched a wooden bridge. Built Army-style, solid and imposing, it reached forty feet across the broken bed of the Palo Blanco. At each end two men patrolled.

On the far side of the river was the fence. There was a gate facing the end of the bridge, perhaps a quarter of a mile from it. The fence stretched as far as Angel could see from this point – perhaps three or four miles of it, seven feet high, glinting in the sunlight.

'I can't see the ranch,' he said.

'We have someway to go yet, Mr Angel,' Denniston replied. 'Quite some way.'

He gigged his horse on down the slope and

approached the two men at the nearer end of the bridge.

'Ho!' one of them shouted. 'Ho, the guard! It's the Colonel!'

They rode past the man in phalanx and Angel tried to conceal his surprise at the way in which each man the Colonel passed snapped to impeccable present-arms, slapping his carbine as if it was an Army Springfield and the man passing in review Phil Sheridan himself.

'Hold it right there, friend,' a voice growled in Angel's ear. He turned to see one of the riders, a thin-faced youngster of perhaps twenty whom he'd noted earlier on account of the two tie-down guns the boy had been sporting, idly cocking a six-shooter which was aimed in the general direction of Angel's midriff.

Angel raised his eyebrows in surprise.

'Nothin' personal, friend,' the kid said. 'The Cunnel just don't like no one peekin' over his shoulder when he opens the gates. One of his little funniosities, you might say.'

'You mean no one can get in or out unless he opens the locks?'

'That's what I mean, sunshine. So don't you go gettin' no ideas about leavin' us, unexpected-like.'

'How do the guards get in and out?'

'Shucks, that'd be tellin' now, wouldn't it?' grinned the kid. He sheathed the gun as he saw

Denniston turn his horse and the gate swing open.

'Let's go, Angel,' he said, and the phalanx moved forward through the gate. Angel covertly checked the fencing as he rode past. It was heavy wire mesh, a quarter of an inch thick, woven into squares about nine inches wide and long. He supposed a man could get through it if he had to. They had said the perimeter was patrolled, though. He could see no one.

Now they were riding through broken country, the trail rising slightly uphill all the time, and ahead Angel could see a gap between two huge shoulders of rock that formed a natural gateway. Presently they were level with this, and again he saw the hidden guards snapping to present arms as their leader rode by. Now, below, he saw the Denniston place, but it was like no ranch he had ever seen. It was laid out on the level of a green and fertile mountain plateau from which every tree and shrub over the height of two feet had been removed, and its rectangular rows of buildings serried on two sides of what looked like a parade ground had the appearance, shape and style of Army buildings. It was not the buildings, though, not the parade ground – if such it was – not yet the bustling figures of many men that he saw which startled Angel. For the place itself lay within yet another fenced area, sentries pacing along its length. As they approached, he saw that there was a gully running laterally across the northern face of the compound where the entrance gate stood flanked by two sentry platforms. Over it ran a footbridge, perhaps six feet wide, with low rails that would not have afforded shelter for a squirrel. As they crossed the bridge, he saw that the gully below was man-made, not natural, and that the smoothed ground bore no trace of a foot or hoof mark.

They rode into the compound, the sentries saluting as Denniston went by, and it was almost exactly like riding into an Army establishment. Squads of men marched by, not drilling, but obviously under some form of disciplined activity. Over in a far corner of the compound seven rows of men under the eye of another were doing punishing gymnastics. Angel looked up as Denniston spoke.

'Angel, come with me. I will want to see all Twos and Threes in twenty minutes,' he added to the others.

'Yes, sir,' they chorused. Angel half expected to see them salute, but they did not. He sought the word for this kind of organisation. They were no guerillas. Not renegades. Yet both. Paramilitary: that was the book-word.

He followed Denniston into the centre building of three on the southern edge of the parade ground. It was sparsely furnished. A simple cot in the corner. A large table with six chairs on either side, a bentwood armchair at its head. A bureau.

Pegs sunk into the walls for hanging hats, clothes, gunbelts. A bearskin rug on the floor. An open hearth with a military sabre crossed on its scabbard above it. A photograph in a silver frame, young men in uniform on a lawn somewhere. And a huge large-scale map of northern New Mexico, southern Colorado and western Kansas on the wall facing the table. A window looked out on to the parade ground.

'Well, Mr Angel?'

'I'm impressed,' Angel said. 'Astonished. But this is no ranch, no way. What are all these men doing up here?'

'I will give you a general answer to your questions, Mr Angel. I cannot be specific until you have been voted by my fellow – ah, officers, to be a man with whom they will serve. This is slightly different to the real Army, but our purpose is such that I can admit of no dissent. Each man has to believe completely in his fellow. There can be no exceptions. However, within the limitations placed upon me by that fact, I will try to satisfy your curiosity.'

'You're raising some kind of Army up here?'

'I suppose you could say that.' Dennison smiled. 'I prefer the term Kommando – a Dutch word meaning a mobile, well-trained, totally ruthless attacking unit.'

'And you use military style and titles?'

'Not quite. You heard outside I asked for Twos

and Threes to join us shortly – when we shall decide upon your acceptability – or otherwise. As commander, I, of course am Number One. There are two Number Twos, of whom the unfortunate Atterbrow was one. Four Number Threes.'

'And how many men?'

'Classified,' Denniston said, smiling slightly to take the sting out of the words. 'I don't wish you to think me discourteous, Mr Angel. But at the moment you have only the status of a possible recruit.'

'And if your – ah, officers don't care to have me along for the ride, what then?'

'Let us hope,' said Denniston without humour, 'that you are not so unlucky.'

He walked across to the window, looking out on the busy scene and lighting a thin cigar which he used as a pointer.

'I've built it all,' he said. 'The whole thing. Slowly, painfully, choosing my location and my men with infinite care. Now . . . now it is almost ready.'

'For what?'

'Ah, Mr Angel, you are a direct man, a man after my own heart. But not even my most trusted subordinates know that.'

Angel shrugged, changing the subject. 'Place like this can't be put together for pennies,' he suggested.

'True,' Dennison said. 'I once owned land. In

Virginia. It was worth a great deal of money. My heritage, you might say. I sold it. Sold that lovely green land for this.' His tone was bitter and his eyes far away, but he got control of himself quickly, as if there had never been gall in his tone. 'And with the passing of time, I found other ways to make money. I made it. And built a little more of my empire. Hired the right men. Paid them enough to keep them happy, keep them loyal. And then began to teach them true loyalty, the loyalty of a man for his own cause, his own Army.' His eyes had gone empty and he was really talking to himself. Angel had ceased to exist except as an excuse to pour out his vanity and contempt.

'Ten years,' Denniston said. 'Ten lost years. But now I am within sight of my objective. Then it will have been worth it.'

Angel walked across the room and picked up the silver-framed photograph from the mantel. Looking at it, he thought one of the faces looked familiar. It was Denniston. A much younger Denniston. He looked up to see the iron-grey eyes watching him.

'You recognised me,' Denniston said.

Angel nodded. 'West Point?'

'Class of '61,' he said. He took the picture from Angel's hands, intoning the names of the faces as his eyes ran over them for the ten thousandth time. 'O'Rourke, Alonzo Cushing, Charles Parsons, Elbert, Jamie Parker, George Custer,

Robley Denniston—' he broke off his reverie, lifting empty eyes towards the window.

'I didn't realise you were Regular Army,' Angel said, for want of anything better to say.

'Yes,' Denniston said dully. 'Yes, I was. I served with George Thomas, General Thomas. At Mill Springs, Murfreeboro, Chickamauga.'

'And then?'

'What? Oh, I was invalided out after Chickamauga. Shot through the lungs. They gave me the usual medals, the usual pension. It wasn't what I wanted. I was used to commanding men. And so I made my plans to do it my own way: If the Army didn't want me, I would build an Army of my own that could not function without me. And I have done it.'

He really believed it, Angel thought. He's convinced himself that it happened that way. The whole dirty little scene after Chickamauga, the court martial and the ignominious discharge have all been safely tucked away where no one can see them.

Denniston went across to the wall where the huge map was hung and looked at it long and intently. There was a red flag stuck into the map on the line which marked the road from Trinidad to Raton through the mountains.

'Well, Mr Angel,' Denniston said, after a while. 'Now you know what the background of this place is. I think we can use you – again providing my

85

staff officers agree. Do you know anything about explosives?'

The question was shot at him without warning and Angel grinned at Dennison without shame.

'Explosives? Where the hell would I learn about explosives? I was too young for your war, Colonel.'

'Quite,' Denniston said. 'It was just a thought.'

'Sure,' Angel said. Before he could say more there was a respectful knock at the door. A man poked his head around it and said that the officers were waiting outside. Denniston nodded and the man closed the door. Denniston motioned Angel to stay where he was and went towards his cot. He pulled a curtain across so that he was hidden behind it. Then, and not until then, the door was smartly opened and five men came into the room. They stood behind their respective chairs alongside the table, their eyes looking up somewhere above head level, faces blank. Then Denniston pulled his curtain aside and stepped into view and the man at the top of the table on the left yelled 'Atteeeeennnnn . . . tion!'

The five men came smartly to attention and saluted, as Denniston sat at the table and said 'At ease, gentlemen.' The quintet sat down in their chairs, hands folded on the table. The man on his left handed Denniston a piece of paper.

'Minutes, sir,' he said.

'Thank you, Froon,' Denniston replied.

Angel watched this imitation of Army ritual in fascinated silence. They were like children playing soldiers, except that they, like Denniston, seemed to believe in it implicitly, and they, like Denniston, intended to use their military force in some way. But what? *What?*

He let his gaze rest on the faces of Denniston's officers one by one. Next to an empty chair on Denniston's right sat the slow-spoken kid who'd held the gun on him at the gate. On his right was a pockmarked man of about thirty with a badly broken noise. On the left hand side of Denniston was the burly man with the wind-burned face who had brought the officers to attention on Denniston's entrance; the other Number Two, Angel guessed. On his left was a tow-haired young man with a Texas drawl who carried a tied-down gun low on his right thigh. And at the end of the table a short, squat, beady-eyed little man who had a singsong accent which Angel finally identified as Welsh. The man looked completely out of place until Angel remembered Denniston's earlier question about explosives. He'd be a miner. And know about things like that.

'Before we discuss business, gentlemen,' Denniston was saying, 'there is the matter of our – ah, guest. And the replacement of John Atterbrow. It is my intention to appoint Mr Angel as a Number Three, replacing John with you, Mr Adam. With the approval of all you gentlemen, of course.'

He looked at them all for a moment, then spoke again.

'Mr Whiting?' That was the miner, who said, 'Agreed sir.'

'Mr Adam?'

'Honoured at my promotion, sir,' drawled the Texan. 'And no objection.'

Denniston nodded.

'Mr Briggs?'

The pockmarked one shook his head. 'Fine with me, sir.'

'And you, Mr Jackson?'

'A question, sir?'

'Certainly.'

'Is Mr Angel any good with that gun?' asked the kid.

Denniston swivelled in his chair and looked at Angel with eyebrow raised.' Well, Mr Angel?'

'I can use it,' Angel said without emphasis. He let his gaze hold that of the younger man until the kid's eyes flickered and evaded it.

Denniston smiled. 'That seems to be that, then. Please join us, Mr Angel. Take Mr Adam's chair. Ray, you move up here beside me.'

Angel sat down in the vacated chair and Denniston looked at the piece of paper in front of him.

'Ah, yes,' he said. 'The first item, Mr Froon: what is the situation?'

'I sent two men down to Vegas,' Froon replied.

'They followed the man and dealt with him. They're waiting to report.'

'Good,' said Denniston, leaning back and steepling his fingers. 'Have they come in.'

Froon got up and went to the door. A thicker man came into the room, his clothes dust-covered, eyes respectful as he came to attention in front of the table.

'Your report, mister!' snapped Froon.

'Me and Rafferty did like you told us, sir. Martinez in the Marshal's office told us that the snooper – beg your pardon, sir, the Government man – was on his way to Fort Union. We trailed him and laid for him about ten miles from Vegas.'

'You killed him?'

'That we did, sir. Deader than a mackerel.'

'Very good, Reed,' Denniston said. 'Was he carrying any papers?'

'Nothing we could find, sir,' Reed said.

'Rafferty was slightly wounded, sir,' Froon put in. 'Nothing serious. Reed brought him back. He's in the sick bay.'

'Good, good,' Denniston said. 'What else did Martinez tell you, Reed?'

'Nothing much else, sir,' Reed said, still standing stiffly to attention and gazing at a point somewhere above Denniston's head. 'Just that this Wells was from the Department of Justice and that he'd sent word back to Washington for another man to come out here.'

Denniston put his hands flat on the table. 'Another Government investigator?'

'That's right, sir,' Reed said. 'Someone called Angel. Frank Angel.'

CHAPTER TEN

Andy Ayres was ten years old.

It wasn't really good fishing weather: too hot. But he called his old dog, Shep, to heel and went off down the creek in the afternoon sunshine, hoping to find a pool somewhere that might have a catfish wallowing in the pool shadows. His fishing rod was a supple willow pole, his bait some chicken bits his mother had given him, and his faith boundless. Shep bounded ahead, happy to be out and free on the open grassland, sniffing away under bushes at the faint remaining scent of prairie chicken or gopher, quartering back across the boy's path, occasionally looking back over his shoulder to make sure his master was still coming.

There was a good pool by the shoulder of the creek bed not far from the road to town that Andy hadn't tried yet, and he headed for this now. He scrambled down the steep shelving bank of the creek and meandered along, picking up pebbles for Shep to chase. As he approached the pool the dog started barking wildly and the boy looked up in alarm. He was frontier bred, and poised if the need arose to run fleet and fast towards the farm – although there hadn't been an Indian scare for the past ten years, his father always drummed vigilance into the boy. There was always danger on the open frontier: he must never take chances. He saw Shep circling around a jumble of rocks, barking wildly at something inside them.

'Shep!' he shouted. 'Come out o' there. What you got, anyway – a gopher?'

The dog took no notice, but went on barking, rushing at the rocks and then backing off warily, dancing from side to side. Andy went nearer, his eyes widening as he saw what looked like a bundle of old clothes thrown among the rocks. Then he realised that the bundle was in fact a man and that the man's chest and back were covered in blood. The man was sitting up – no, trying to sit up would have been a more accurate description. He was trying to say something, but the boy could not make out what it was. He was very frightened and did not know whether to go nearer or run away. His father's stern warnings came back to him but his curiosity was stronger: he went nearer. The man saw him and leaned back against the rocks his face streaming with sweat, twisted with pain.

'Boy,' the man said. 'Boy.'

92

'What's the matter, mister?' Andy said. 'You hurt? Who are you?'

'Boy,' the man said again. 'Water.'

He made a little gesture with his arm, and Andy realised the man was badly hurt, maybe dying. He was frightened again.

'Please,' the man said.

Andy ran down to the creek where there was a slow trickle of clear mountain water. Then he realised he had nothing to carry the water in. He ran back to see if the man had a hat.

'Water,' the man said again. His voice was fainter.

'You got to come to where the water is,' Andy told him. 'Can't you walk?'

'Water,' the man said. 'Walk.'

Andy just looked at him. There was nothing he could do. The man was too heavy for him to lift. He didn't know what to do. He wished his father was here.

'Wait,' he said to the man. He went closer to him, gingerly touching the man's arm. 'Wait here. I'll get help. Wait here.' The man looked at him through eyes washed pale by pain. But he seemed to understand. He nodded.

'Wait,' he said. 'Get help.'

'That's right, mister,' the boy said, and turned and ran as if all the devils in Hell were chasing him, the dog bounding along beside him, running ahead and barking as Andy scooted fleet-footed across the burned plain along the side of the creek, then bore right and up the path towards his home, running, running, running until he saw his father and ran to him shouting 'Pa, Pa, Pa!'

John Ayres was a big man with muscles corded from years of hard work on the little farm in the fold of the hills. He ran towards his son, snatching up the pistol and belt that hung always close to him as he worked.

The boy blurted out his discovery and Ayres frowned, buckling the belt on as Andy spoke. His wife came out of the house, having heard the boy's excited voice, and Ayres quickly told her what had happened.

'Stay here with your mother, boy,' he told his son, and when Andy made a moue of disappointment, went on, 'Someone's got to look after her.' His words brought a quick smile of pride to the youngster's face.

'I'll go down there and take a look, Martha,' he said. 'Maybe you'd better get a tub of hot water ready. If what Andy says is true, this man's bad hurt.'

He strode off without another word, a tall dark man moving purposefully across his own land, the dog loping beside him through the scrubby grass and sagebrush. Within ten minutes he was beside the wounded man, dipping his neckerchief in the creek and bathing his bitten lips.

'Thanks,' Wells said. 'Thank you.'

He started to talk and Ayres bade him be silent.

'Talk all you like when I get you back to the house,' he said. 'Right now you better save your strength. From the look of that hole in your back you're going to need it.'

Angus Wells was not a small man nor a light one, and he was too weak to give the tall farmer any real help. But John Ayres picked him up as if he was a baby, and got Wells across his shoulder. Wells cried out once and then collapsed into unconsciousness. Ayres nodded as though obscurely pleased by this fact, and then strode off back towards his house, covering the ground in good long strong strides, his wife coming to the door as she saw her husband approaching with the burden. They got Wells into the house and Mrs Ayres stripped away the bloody shirt with a butcher knife. She pulled the breath sharply between her lips as she saw Wells' wounds.

'John,' she said. 'This is work for a doctor. If the man doesn't get medical help, he'll die.'

'You're right as usual, Martha,' John Ayres said. 'Andy, you go out and harness the mare. I'll take the wagon. With luck I can be in Vegas before nightfall. Come, help me, love. We'll at least wash his wounds and bandage them before he has to travel. It's a bad road.'

Two hours later, John Ayres swung his wagon out on to the road, and by late afternoon he had reached Las Vegas. It was only a small place, huddled around the tree-shaded plaza, its old streets narrow, dusty, crowded. Women were standing near the fountain, gossiping. They looked up incuriously as the *Anglo* drove past with his wagon. John Ayres was a familiar figure in the town. He pulled up outside a brick building three doors down the street from the offices which housed the local newspaper, the *Optic*. A wooden sign jutted from the wall, its paint faded by many years of sun. Ayres recalled when it had been fresh and golden, eight years ago when Jack Cox had come to town. He was an ambitious young doctor then. Now he was just a doctor. He had found his vocation in Las Vegas, no child ever needed to suffer pain or sickness if Cox could help. The Mexicans rarely had money. When they could, they paid. When they had nothing, he treated them anyway. Ayres happened to think he was a very fine human being, but of course they had never been able to talk about things like that. He pushed into the office and explained quickly why he had come. Within ten minutes Wells was lying on the long leather-covered table in the back room, while Cox surveyed his wounds with a practised eye that did not miss any of the other scars on Wells' body.

'Led an active life, this one,' he said, stripping away the bandages Ayres' wife had wound around Wells' body. 'Martha did a good job, John. As usual. Who is he, do you know?'

'We didn't try to ask him questions,' Jack Ayres said. 'He was out most of the time anyway.'

'Hmm,' said Cox. He got a bottle of sal ammoniac from the bag and waved it under Wells' nose. After a minute or two, Wells flinched from the bottle, his eyes flickering.

'That's the boy,' cooed Cox. He waved the bottle around again and this time Wells opened his eyes.

'Where—' he said, trying to sit up. Cox restrained him with a firm hand.

'Easy, now,' he said. 'Don't you go getting excited.'

Wells nodded. 'You a doctor?' Cox inclined his head, and Wells asked a question.

'You're in my office in Las Vegas,' the doctor said. 'This is John Ayres, who found you and brought you here.'

'I'm – I don't know how—'

'Ach, no need of that,' Ayres said. 'What's your name, man? What happened to you?'

Wells told them his name and what he was, told them what had happened to him on the road and his suspicions about the reason for the ambush. They listened without speaking, and then Cox said, 'You'll be wanting us to get word to Fort Union, then?'

Wells nodded. 'Most urgent,' he whispered. 'Matter of life and death.'

'Whose, laddie?' Cox said, wryly. 'Theirs – or yours?'

Wells didn't answer. He had fallen back on the bed, out again. But Cox looked at his friend.

'Was he telling the truth, do you think?'

'Why would he make up a story like that, Jack?'

'Why indeed,' Cox said. 'All right, John – get yourself out of here. I've serious work to do. I'll try and patch up our friend so that he'll hold together until they can send an ambulance down from the Fort. If you go down the street and see Pedro Chavez y Chavez, he'll send one of his boys over to the Fort. You can write some kind of note for him to take, can't you?'

'I can do that,' Ayres agreed. 'And I will. But what abut Wells? Will he live?'

'Aye, he'll live, John,' Cox said. 'Whether he'll like it when he finds out his spine has a bullet lodged against it, I'm not so sure.'

'What does that mean?'

'I wish I had the knowledge and the equipment to tell you the answer to that, John,' the doctor said. 'A fifty-fifty chance he'll never walk again.'

He looked down at his patient and stifled a curse as he realised that Wells had regained consciousness and had been listening to every word he said.

'Hell,' he said hastily, 'I don't know anything, of course. I'm more than likely completely wrong. Lie still, there, now. John, won't you get on and arrange that other business. Go on, go on, go on,' he ranted on, bustling the big man out of the room, making a big show of sorting out his instruments and washing his hands, avoiding the eyes of the man on the bed. Finally he turned to face Wells and his eyes widened with surprise when he saw that Wells was grinning.

'This is no damned laughing matter, you know,' he said, mock-angry, alarmed lest perhaps Wells was becoming delirious or might even have tetanus. God, what he'd give for proper equipment!

'Take it easy, Doc,' Wells said. 'Take it easy. Five hours ago I was as near dead as a man can be. Now you're giving me a fifty-fifty chance. I reckon by tomorrow morning I'll be up and around at this rate.'

Cox looked at his patient with new respect.

'By God,' he muttered. 'It wouldn't surprise me at all.'

CHAPTER ELEVEN

'Well, well, well,' Denniston said.

You had to hand it to him, Angel thought. He didn't blow his cool at all – just a slight rise of the eyebrows and even, perhaps, a hint of a smile at the corners of the patrician mouth.

It was the kid, Jackson, who reacted. He was on his feet in an instant, the chair going over backwards away from him as he faced Angel across the table, his hand poised over the tied-down gun. The tableau froze: nobody moved.

'All right, you treacherous bastard!' snapped the kid. 'You said you could use your gun. Let's see you do it!'

Angel looked at Denniston, who returned his gaze blandly. Frank Angel shrugged and cocked the gun he was holding beneath the table. The kid heard it and his face went white.

'That's right,' Angel told him.

He let them all think about it for a moment, then spoke again. 'The gun I'm holding under the table is loaded with soft-nosed bullets, and each one of them has a cross cut into it,' he lied. 'I hope I don't need to give you a detailed description of what would happen to any of your bellies if I were to cut loose with it.'

He let them think about that, his own mind racing. Getting the drop on the men in this room was one thing. Getting out of the building and then out of the compound was something else again. It might have been that some of this showed on his face, for Denniston smiled and spoke, laying his hands flat on the table and leaning forward carefully, so as not to precipitate violence.

'Put the gun on the table, Mr Angel,' he said. 'There is no way you can get out of here alive.'

'He's telling you the truth, *bach*,' the man on Angel's left said.

'Sure,' Angel replied. He got up and pushed his own chair back, his eyes watching all of them for any sudden move. But with the exception of the kid, who still stood looking as if he would like to go for his gun, the men around the table looked relaxed – as though they had no wish or need to try to prevent his escape.

'Listen to me, Angel,' Denniston said. 'Just listen.'

'Talk away,' Angel said. He eased over to the window, taking in the layout of the compound, adding what he could see to the mental map he had drawn on his first arrival. He knew without looking that there were buildings on each side of the one he was in: Quarters for the 'officers' of Denniston's 'army'. He was facing north: the gate and its bridged ditch lay straight ahead. Off to the right was a stone building, the south wall of which was sandbagged and reinforced with timber to take the impact of the bullets fired at the targets standing before it – the rifle range. On the western side of the compound stood six barracks and in the far north-western corner he knew there was a high wire-mesh compound that housed patrol dogs – Alsatians, he had guessed. All this he took in swiftly, his gaze checking off the number of men in the square outside, the distance involved, the odds for and against the several plans that came into his mind to be immediately discarded.

'If you should get across the parade ground to the gate – which is highly doubtful – you have to cross the bridge. There are four guards on the bridge day and night and two guards in each of the vedettes flanking the gate. Let us suppose,' Denniston droned relentlessly on, 'you even managed somehow to get past the guards and over the bridge, you would be in no-man's land. The trail you came in here on is the only way in or out. If you step off it, you will be in no-man's land. There are trip wires linked to explosives buried everywhere out there, Angel. There are man-traps hidden beneath soft sand, under bushes – they would take the hoof off a horse and certainly cripple a man. Let us suppose, however, that you neither hit a tripwire nor stumbled into one of the traps, you would be alone in the wilderness, your wits and your pistol all you would have to sustain you. I, however, would send a hundred men out to find you, hunt you down, kill you. The dogs in the compound are man killers. They can find you in land where an Apache would lose a trail. There is no way out, Angel. Put down your gun.'

'Very convincing,' Angel said. 'I almost believe you.'

Denniston threw up his hands in a gesture of near-disgust. 'I thought you were an intelligent man, Angel,' he said. 'Instead, I see that you're a fool. Very well, I wash my hands of you.'

Angel raised the window. It moved easily on its sash cords. When it was open about three feet, he bent in one smooth movement and stepped on to the ramada outside the building. As he did Ray Adam stood up and in the same moment flipped the gun he had drawn beneath the table level, easing back the hammer and letting fly as Angel stepped swiftly to one side, moving fast across the face of the building and down the alley between it and the officers' quarters adjacent, running flat out as he heard shouts and the sound of running feet crunching on the gravel of the parade ground. Ahead of him reared the high wire fence.

It looked enormous, unscalable, but he thrust the pistol into his holster and ran at the fence, using the vaulting-horse technique they had taught him in the gymnasium in Washington. His left hand acted as a pivot, gripping the wire about his own shoulder height, hurling his body flat on to the wire, and arcing on the pivot of the hand like someone vaulting a stile, the powerful surge of run and whipcorded muscle taking his right leg across the top strand of the wire, the jagged ends tearing into his skin as he switched his weight over and then dropped down to the far side. Men came skidding around the corner of the building and saw him. He heard one of them shout something and threw a shot towards them, the slug aimed high to make them hunt cover rather than to kill. They dived to both sides of the alley, getting as near to the walls of the buildings as they could.

'Come back!' he heard someone shout. 'Come back!'

He threw another shot at the sound just for luck and then turned and hunted cover down the steep side of a low shelf that overhung a thin wash perhaps fifteen yards from the wire. He whirled sharp left, moving up the wash towards the west, where the peaked edges of the divide above Kiowa reared sharp against the sky. He was thinking about the climb up there when he hit the trip-wire and the world blew up in his face.

*

Angel surveyed his prison.

It was a square stone room, with a barred window set high on the wall opposite his bed. There was a table with a tin washbowl on it, a chair. Into the right hand wall was set a massive wood door with a judas window. He could hear the sounds of men marching on the parade ground outside. He eased his position in the bed and winced. Every muscle of his body ached. He felt as if he had been stepped on by some gigantic monster. His hands were bandaged. He had no mirror so did not know that his face was lacerated and that most of his body was one solid bruise. They had come out and carried him in unconscious, every shred of his clothing tattered and ripped by the flat hard force of the explosion that had been set off when he hit the tripwire. He grimaced, and tried to sit up. The world swam and he fell back on the cot, panting.

Great, he thought.

After a while he tried again. This time the dizziness was not so bad and he was able to sit up and then swing his legs down to the floor. He was sweating as if he had lifted heavy loads for an hour. No good. He wasn't in any condition to go anywhere yet. He went across and dragged the chair towards the wall, standing on it to look out of the window. There seemed to be a lot of activity outside. The men were being assembled, horses being led across the parade ground, orders shouted. He heard footsteps in the passageway outside the door of his cell and stepped down quickly from the chair, putting it back beside the table and sitting down. The judas window slid aside and he saw someone look in. Then keys ratted in the lock. The door swung inwards and Denniston stepped into the room.

'Well, Mr Angel,' he said. 'I see you're up and about.'

The prisoner said nothing. He just looked at Denniston expressionlessly.

'Well,' Denniston said, unabashed by the silence, 'I thought I would bid you farewell. I'm afraid I shall not be able to witness your execution.'

'You're breaking my heart,' Angel said. 'What execution is this?'

'Tomorrow, at sunrise,' he was told, 'you will be taken from here and shot. I have no further use for you. It is mere chance that you were not killed in your foolish escape bid. Since, however, you were not, then we shall execute you according to military procedure.'

Angel sneered, letting the contempt he felt for this nonsense show on his face. He desperately wanted to put Denniston off-balance, jar the man into self-exposure. But Denniston wasn't having any.

'Think what you like,' he said. 'You'll be shot anyway.'

'First Wells, now me,' Angel said. 'You think you can take on the entire United States Department of Justice?'

Denniston threw back his head and laughed, and for the first time Angel caught the note of incipient madness in it.

'You stupid fool!' Denniston snapped. 'You have no conception of the size of my plans!'

'Tell me, then,' Angel said softly. 'What exactly are your plans?'

Denniston looked at his prisoner for a long moment and then nodded, as if coming to a decision.

'I suppose you ought to have some recompense for dying so young,' he said. 'Perhaps I shall tell you.' His burning eyes fastened on Angel's, there was a haunted look far back in them.

'Tell me,' he said, 'were you in the War?'

'In a way,' Angel said.

'But not the Army?'

'No. Not the Army.'

'Ah,' said Denniston, as if that explained everything. 'Then you have never seen a man being drummed out of camp?'

Angel shook his head. 'That what they did to you?'

The burning eyes widened a fraction, and then a wicked smile touched Denniston's lips.

'Ah, yes,' he said softly. 'You'd know about that, of course. The knowledge seals my intent more strongly than ever, now you have to die, Angel.'

'We all have to die,' Angel said. 'Even you, Denniston.'

The man shook his head, the evil smile lingering at the corners of his thin lips.

'I have been dead for many years,' he said. 'Many years. Let me tell you about how I died, Angel. It was not the physical death that all men seem to fear, oh, no. It was the death of the spirit that is more cruel, more agonising than any wound inflicted by bullet or knife. The death of the spirit,' he repeated. His eyes were vacant, as if his thoughts were far away. 'You see, what they do if you show you are afraid in battle is so obscene, so vile, that you can hardly understand what is happening to you. They assemble all the officers, and strip your uniform off you, button by button, badge by badge. They snap your sword. They revile you openly, disavow you publicly. Then four soldiers with fixed bayonets are placed behind you as guards and they march you through the camp, the fifes and drums playing. The fifes and drums playing.' He faltered, hearing in his mind the drone of the 'Rogue's March' and feeling the rough poking pricks of the bayonets in the hands of the jeering soldiers, stumbling across the camp ground with his eyes blind with tears, every man in the entire regiment hooting, jeering, cursing.

'The fifes and drums?' Angel said softly.

'Uh?' Denniston's head snapped up. 'Oh. Yes. No matter. I prefer not to discuss it further. Let us simply say that I could never, ever forgive the men who disgraced me that day. The man who above all others was responsible for treating me – me, who had fought with honour a dozen major battles, more – like a slinking cur. I was drummed out, Mister Angel. Drummed out. A West Pointer. Do you know what kind of death that is?'

Angel shook his head. The kind of pride the military had was one he had never attempted to understand. It had to do with passing examinations and family connections and knowing the right people and never getting your copybook blotted and seemed anyway like a hell of a way for a man to spend his life. He said none of this, however.

'Now I have my own army,' Denniston said. 'Trained men. You have seen the results of their training.'

'The raids on the Army posts,' Angel said. 'The ambush of the wagon train? You could have used renegade Apaches and got the same result. Trained men only kill when they have to, not gratuitously like mad dogs.'

'No, no,' Denniston held up his hand in remonstrance.

'No, they killed those men under my orders. It was imperative that no one who had seen us, no one who threatened our eventual mission was to be allowed to live. That is why your colleague was killed. Why you will be killed. Why anyone who stands in my way will be killed.'

His voice had risen slightly, and he was breathing faster, as if angered by his own words, moved by a sort of self-hypnotism.

'Your eventual mission?'

'Ah, yes,' Denniston said, his calm returning. 'I promised you, did I not? Well, my digression had point, although it may have puzzled you. Tonight my men and I ride out of here. We will take the guns we – ah – liberated and the ammunition. And, of course, the Gatling gun.' He shook his head in self-admiration. 'A stroke of pure genius, that, I think. Well. Tonight we march. We march to – a destination I think I shall not reveal to you. Mister Angel, although it is not a long way away. There we shall prepare for a battle. Along both sides of a canyon my men will be lying in wait, those beautifully accurate Army weapons aimed and ready, the Gatling gun loaded and carefully located where its lethal firepower can do the most damage. And down that canyon will come the man who gave the order to have me drummed out of the camp at Chickamauga ten years ago – the man who is now President of the United States, Ulysses Simpson Grant!'

His words hung in the still air like some

monstrous black bird. Angel reacted the only way he knew how.

'You're insane,' he said.

Just for a second the fires of madness consumed the brain behind the glaring, iron-grey eyes. Denniston's hand swept across in a tight arc.

'Damn your impudent soul, sir!' he screamed, as his open hand slapped Angel off the chair and sent him sprawling on the floor. The door burst inwards and a guard stood behind Denniston, revolver cocked, eyes taking in the whole scene in one sweeping glance.

'It's all right,' Denniston panted, drawing himself upright. The man gawped at him and Denniston's voice went up a register. 'Get out!'

'Yessir,' gasped the guard, retreating hastily and closing the door behind him. Angel got slowly to his feet, sitting on the bed and leaning against the wall. The room slowly stopped spinning around and he focused on his captor, realising Denniston was talking again.

'You will remember to whom you are speaking, Angel!' Denniston said coldly, his iron self-control fully reasserted now. 'I hold your life in this hand—' he held a clenched fist forward— 'and should I order it, you would die in the room right now. Hold on to your last few hours of life, and savour them. As I shall do.'

He turned and knocked on the door. The guard opened it and Denniston went out. As he did, he turned. There was an ironic smile on his face.

'Reflect upon the word insane, Mister Angel,' he said, flatly. 'Am I insane who can and will do exactly as I said I will? Or are you and your puny civil service heroes insane to try and stop me?' He looked at the guard, who grinned obligingly, and then the door slammed into place. Frank Angel sat on the cot in the stone prison room and stared at the wall. In two hours it would be sundown. On present indications he had almost twelve hours to live. Right now he was hardly strong enough to knock down a self-respecting pigeon.

He looked at his trembling hands and grimaced.

Twelve hours.

CHAPTER TWELVE

At around four in the morning Angel made his move.

He had heard the preparations for departure outside, the tinny sound of the bugles blowing assembly and the men running to meet their horse-handlers, taking the reins and swinging into the saddles moving out in a solid phalanx with the Gatling gun swinging on its spindly-looking wheels behind the team pulling it. Nightfall had brought a deep silence to the compound, as if the very mountains around it were huddled closer to shield it from prying outsiders. Once in a while Angel heard the guard (guards?) outside his cell coughing, or humming a few bars of 'Lorena'. Towards midnight he could hear someone snoring. He edged his chair towards the window and watched the darkness outside until his eyes could make out the thicker, blacker shapes of men moving in the compound. There were still guards on the gates and in the vedettes above. How many? Were there any patrols on the fence? If so, where? And again, how many? He smiled grimly in the blackness. He'd find out soon enough.

Now it was time. He sat down on the cot and prepared his weapons. Although Denniston's men had taken his guns and searched him thoroughly, they had not discovered the things which were the result of the hours Angel had spent alone with the Armourer, discussing ways in which a man could carry undetected weapons and what those weapons might be. They should, preferably, be weapons which killed silently and efficiently. The man should also have weapons which might double as tools. The tools and weapons should be very light but enormously strong, and they should be capable of concealment in places which would not normally attract attention during a search. The Armourer in the Justice Department building had grinned at Angel's insistence.

'You don't want much, do you?' he had said.

'It's my life,' Angel had reminded him. 'I want the best there is.'

'See what we can to,' the Armourer had promised. And a few days later, Angel had received a message telling him to go down to the echoing basement on the Tenth Street side of the building, and the Armourer had met him with a wide grin.

'Think I've got what you want,' he said, and held out a pair of ordinary riding boots and a wide belt with a heavy brass buckle. Angel looked at them and then at the Armourer.

'They're your size,' the Armourer said. 'Try them on.'

And then he had seen the weapons. Inside the belt lying neatly in a groove scoured into the rough leather, looped a thin wire at both of whose ends were two flat wooden pegs, perhaps two inches long.

'Garrotte,' the Armourer had nodded. 'Now the buckle.'

The buckle was in two pieces which clipped together. When separated one of them became a razor-edged knife whose wicked edge was covered by the overlaying decorative buckle when placed back on the belt.

'Pretty snaky,' Angel said, grinning. 'How about the boots?'

They were straightforward mule-ear boots with a stitched pattern that was in no way unconventional. The Armourer showed him where on the outside flap – the long strip used for pulling on the boots which gave them their name of 'mule-ears' – the outer leather and the softer inner were slightly separated. Inside each scabbard thus formed nestled two flat-bladed throwing knives, perfectly balanced, their blades widening into tulip-head shapes and then wicked points.

'Solingen steel,' the Armourer said. 'From Germany. Best there is. Just like you asked for.' He grinned mischievously and then spent another hour or so with Angel showing him the best way to use the knives, throwing over-handed or under, flicking them out from the boot and up, until he pronounced himself satisfied.

And these were the weapons with which Angel must now make his desperate bid for freedom. The odds were enormous, he knew. But there was no alternative. Somehow word had to be passed through to the President. Whatever it was, whatever he was doing, it must be something that would bring him within marching distance of the mountain stronghold. Some canyon. But where, where?

Angel stood up and flexed his arms. His body still felt stiff and overused, but there was no time to think of that any more. He slid on his boots and kicked the door, hard, yelling wordlessly. And he went on kicking and yelling until he saw the judas window slide back but now he was on the floor at the foot of the door, still screaming mindlessly and banging on the door with his boots.

'Shut up in there!' yelled the man outside. 'Shut up, damn you!'

Angel went on making as much noise as his throat and lungs could manufacture, hammering his heels against the door and ignoring the curses and commands of the man on the other side of it.

After a few minutes he heard the sound he had been hoping for, the man's keys scrabbling in the lock of the door, and as the door pushed inwards, he rolled away from it and came up along its edge, hands looping the garrotte neatly over the thick throat of the advancing guard. It was a nasty way to kill a man but Angel closed his mind to that. He clamped the man's flailing arms with his own elbows, twisting the wire tighter, tighter, tighter, choking with nausea as the dying man's sphincter muscle relaxed and his body voided itself, pulling the man back now and down on to the dirty floor, all of this taking minutes, his body drenched in sweat, lymphets of fatigue dancing before his eyes.

'Charlie?' someone shouted. Then '*Charlie?*'

Angel tore the biting wire loose from the man's throat and stepped over the body, his hand ready as the man shouted 'Charlie, what the hell?'

The man was a big, chunky fellow who stepped into the corridor, his mouth full of apple, the fruit in his hand. His jaws fell open at the sight of Angel in the doorway and his brain flashed a command that the body never got a chance to obey. Angel threw the flat-bladed knife in his right hand, snapping the arm down on the last part of the throw to give the weapon that penetration it would otherwise not have. The knife winked once in the lamplighted corridor and buried itself to the hilt in the throat of the man

117

with the apple. He gave a horrible choking cry and lurched back against the wall, bright red blood spurting from the wound in his neck and splashing the ground and the rough stones as the man fell silently, dead as he hit the floor. Angel was beside him even as the man gave one long last sighing moan and slid all the way down to deep and ending death, sliding the knife out with a rough flick of the wrist, wiping it callously on the dead man's clothing. He was in the outer room of the 'Punishment Block' as he had heard them jokingly call it. There were guns and carbines in a cabinet behind the desk where the man with the apple had been sitting. Two cups of coffee steamed on the table. Angel gulped one of them, the hot liquid warming his chilled body. He opened the cupboard and took out a new-lookin Peacemaker, its 7" barrel nearest to the kind of weight and balance he had gotten used to from using an old Army Colt. Stuffing his pockets with ammunition, he scanned the other weapons in the cabinet and finally took down a shotgun whose barrels had been sawn off. It was a ten-gauge, and he found ammunition in a box behind it. This wicked weapon gave him for the first time hope that he might just make it out of the compound. The sawn-off shotgun was a terrible weapon: eighteen 00 buckshot – blue whistlers, some called them – could literally cut a man in half at close range, and – Angel grinned wolfishly as he thought it – sure as hell didn't do anything for the health of anyone within twenty or thirty yards of the barrel. He broke the gun, loaded it, sliding the Peacemaker into his belt. He didn't want to start shooting until he had to, and so he fashioned a loop for the shotgun out of a thin leather strap that belonged to the case of a pair of field glasses. With the shotgun now hanging from his left shoulder, Angel eased back the door of the Punishment Block and looked out on to the deserted parade ground. There were no lights in the barracks, but one or two burned in the big building where he had been exposed by the man who had killed Angus Wells. Angel's mouth went grim and thin at the thought: he would have a reckoning with Mister Ed Reed in due course.

He eased silently across the front of the cell building and then down the side furthest from the gate, cutting in front of the tattered board cut-outs standing in front of the sandbags on the firing range. He froze as he heard a footfall crunch on loose stone somewhere near the perimeter fence. He had kept his eyes half closed until now to hasten night vision. Now he let them open wide and picked the man up quickly. He was standing in the open, idling, not hurrying to complete his circuit of the fence. Angel watched as the man scratched himself and yawned. Then the man hoisted his Springfield off the ground and with the weapon at trail walked dawdling towards the shadowed rear of the Punishment Block. As soon as he reached the darkness, Angel moved. It was literally only three yards from his hiding place to where the man was walking, and Angel covered them before the man had time to whirl around or cry out. The seeking knife held rigid in Angel's left hand found the lower ribs and slid upwards, severing the aorta even as Angel's right hand clamped on the man's mouth and racked his head back, Angel's knee ramming into the base of the man's spine, smashing him back and down dead on the ground. It hardly made a sound. Now Angel picked up the Springfield, and with it at trail himself walked slowly along the perimeter fence, turning left as he reached the right angle on the north-east corner, coming up to the gates and beneath the vedette tower on the right hand side. There were two men guarding the gate. One of them looked up as Angel came nearer.

'Hey, Tom,' he said. Then, 'Tom?'

That was all the warning Angel was going to get and he knew it, so when the man's hand stabbed for the gun in its holster, he flicked the Peacemaker up and shot the man through the head. The shot baroomed like thunder in the darkness as the second guard got his gun into action, trying to hit the now-rolling form of Angel, who had thrown himself to the ground the moment after firing the shot which had killed the first. Dust spurted up, and Angel felt the bullets slam into the ground and he fired through the dusty darkness and saw the second guard go backwards, clutching his belly, down over the edge of the bridge across the ditch outside the gate. Now the two vedettes were at the parapets, searching the ground below as Angel scuttled to the dark shadows at the foot of the fence. He could hear men shouting at the far side of the parade ground, and the dogs in the compound were barking furiously at the noise.

'Where the hell is he, Willie?' one of the guards above shouted. Angel rolled over on his back, his arm across his face to conceal its paler shade, and saw the men hurrying down the ladders of the towers, two from the side nearest him, one from the other. With a savage grin he rolled forward and on to one knee. One of the men shouted 'There he is!' and then Angel cut loose with the shotgun. The man who had shouted was torn off his feet by the first barrel, the nine double-zeroes whacking him seven feet to one side, his body cut to bits by the whistling buckshot. Even as the tattered body was falling, Angel swung the gun around and blasted the second man down, blowing him against the wire fence so hard that the wire acted as a trampoline and hurled the man hard away and down on his face, limbs and trunk as limp as those of a rag doll. The third man,

121

firing hastily and without aim as he ran, saw the other two suddenly smashed down and tried to turn and run but instead got tangled up in his own confusion and fell to the ground in front of Angel, about fifteen yards away. He tried to raise the gun and his expression when the hammer clicked on an empty chamber was totally comical.

'Some days nothing goes right, does it?' Angel grinned and laid the long barrel of the Peacemaker alongside the man's head, just above the ear. The man went down into the dirt like a bundle of old clothes. Now there were men coming out of the buildings and running across the parade ground and Angel slid two more of the red buckshot cartridges into the breech of the shotgun, pulling both triggers almost casually, the buckshot screeching into the advancing cluster of men, who slewed aside in panic as they saw the flash and heard the dull boom of the gun. One man went over, his legs kicking high in agony, and another let loose a high thin piercing scream as one of the double-zeroes smashed into his elbow and mangled the joint into a jelly of bloody tissue and bone. Even as the men scattered, Angel was quartering across the open ground towards the stables, one or two of the scattered men behind him firing blindly into the darkness where he had been, shouting confused orders to each other which nobody obeyed.

Inside the dark stable, Angel grabbed the

halter of a big lineback dun and led him outside
into the open, the shotgun in his right hand
again loaded. He felt rather than saw the man
coming up on his right and heard the man shout
'Get him, boys!' and knew the man had turned
one of the dogs loose – *how many of them were there?*
– and then he heard the dark deep growl of the
dog as it launched itself at him and in pure reflex
pulled both triggers of the shotgun. The dog was
torn to ribbons by the terrible force of the shot at
such close quarters and fell in a quivering, smok-
ing heap of bloody meat to one side of him. The
man came rushing at Angel in the wake of the
dog, and Angel let him come, one hand still holding the rope halter. The man raised his gun and
fired but the hasty shot missed. Then Angel
whirled in a tight half-circle and hit the man
across the bridge of the nose with the shotgun.
The man fell to his knees mewling through the
broken bones of his face and Angel hit him again,
a savage felling blow with the heavy gun that flattened the man to the ground. Without waiting to
see whether the man would move, Angel swung
aboard the horse and kicked it into a gallop,
pulling its head around towards the gate.
Someone shouted from the shelter of the alleys
between the barracks and he emptied the
Peacemaker in that direction, his shots driving
the men there back to cover as he thundered
across the wooden footbridge and down the trail,

the sounds of shots falling behind him, the night enveloping him, the rustling wind cold on his face. There was still the outer fence, he told himself grimly. Still more guards. He eased the horse to a canter, gripping the rope halter between his teeth as he slid cartridges into the Peacemaker and again loaded the shotgun. About a mile below him he could see the dark outline of the Palo Blanco canyon. Faint pink streaks were leaving the blackness of the sky. It would soon be dawn. Now he saw the outer fence, remembering as he did the way Denniston had opened the gates while all the others had hung back.

He rode the horse up to the gate and hitched it to the wire fence ten feet away. On foot, he ran across to the centre of the gates where the flat metal lock held the two steel uprights close and tight. Without ado he thrust the barrels of his shotgun against the lock, turned his face and body half away and pulled the triggers. The shotgun boomed and was torn out of his hand by the close recoil, but the lock, mangled and broken, fell apart and the gates swung open. He ran back towards the horse as someone shouted down by the bridge across the Palo Blanco

'Hey, you!' the man shouted. He was running, porting a rifle, not sure what was happening until he saw Angel coming at him on horseback, and then he dropped quickly to one knee and took aim. He fired at the same instant as Angel, but he was shooting uphill and did not lead enough. His slug went whining off into infinity as the bullet from Angel's Peacemaker slapped him aside, his tumbling body going off the side of the steep canyon wall and down into the boulder-strewn bottom. Angel kicked the horse into a gallop on to the bridge as the second guard came running forward, levelling a sixgun which he thumbed twice, his slugs whipping past Angel as Angel launched himself off the back of the horse, his whole body and the speed at which he had been coming making him a projectile that smashed the man to the ground, the sixgun flying from nerveless hands. The two men rolled over and over on the wooden boards, the guard desperately trying to get some kind of grip on the body of his assailant. Locked together, the two men rolled about, their legs seeking purchase on the rough boards. They struggled to their knees, the guard's thumbs gouging towards Angel's eyes in a desperate attempt to blind his opponent, grunting with the effort, his face contorted with rage and the lust to kill. Then Angel relaxed, let go, rolled over backwards, bringing the guard with him, his right knee lifting the man slightly as the momentum of the rolling fall brought the man above him. Then Angel snapped his leg straight and the man went over and up, as if his head were a pivot on which he was turning, and came down flat and tremendously hard on his back, his head to Angel's head. Angel was on his feet even as the man hit the ground, the edge of his right hand extended now slightly forward as the guard scrabbled to his feet, winded, his eyes wary now and frightened. He made an inarticulate noise in his throat and rushed at Angel, who swayed to one side and then hit the man at the base of his right ear with the calloused edge of his right hand. The man smashed face down, hands clawing at the wooden boards in pain, and Angel was behind him, astraddle the man's back, the barrel of the Peacemaker jammed into the base of the guard's neck.

'Denniston,' he said. 'Which way did he go?'

'Go to hell!' spat the guard.

Angel cocked the sixgun and repeated the question, getting the same answer.

'I haven't got time for this,' Angel said reasonably, and shot the top of the man's right ear. The roar of the sixgun and the searing pain brought a terrified scream from the man, who bucked and fought against Angel's weight on his back.

'One more time,' Angel said grimly. 'Which way?'

'West,' groaned the man. 'Through the mountains above Kiowa.'

'Where's he heading?'

'I don't know,' the guard said.

Angel cocked the Peacemaker again.

'Sweartogodsthetruth, mister!' screeched the guard. 'Nobody knew where they was goin'. The Colonel, he was the only one knew!'

Angel lifted himself off the prone man and stood back, allowing the man to get to his feet.

'How many men with him?' he asked.

'Forty, fifty, something like that,' he man said. 'You goin' after him, mister?'

'Something like that,' Angel parroted.

'He'll kill you for sure, when he sees you,' the guard said. Some of his confidence was coming back. He touched the wounded ear and winced, looking at the blood on his fingers and then up at Angel with hate in his eyes.

'I hope he shoots your balls off,' he said venomously.

'That's a thought,' Angel said equably. As he spoke he moved the Peacemaker in a short arc, the barrel flashing in the dawning sunshine and smacking the guard, who was too surprised to move, alongside his unwounded ear. He fell to his knees like a poleaxed steer, his mouth agape, eyes rolling up in his head.

'Sleep warm,' Angel said, and hit him again.

CHAPTER THIRTEEN

'End of the line, Mister President.'

Grant's aide came into the plush parlour of the railroad carriage which the President used on his cross-country trips and saluted.

Grant looked up from the copy of the St Louis *Democrat* he was reading, the cigar cocked as always in the right hand corner of his mouth. He acknowledged the salute with a nod and heaved himself off the comfortable seat.

'Well, we've had our pleasure, gentlemen,' he said to the other three men sitting opposite him, 'and now we must work for our vittles.'

They all smiled with varying degrees of uncomfortableness. Grant was a man who loved to get his backside into a McClellan and pound across this godforsaken wilderness for hours. Grant would cheerfully pitch a tent and spend the night out on the plains or in the mountains, happy to sit by a big fire of buffalo chips and swig from a bottle of Irish whiskey. A gentleman, however, (which they all privately agreed Grant was not and never would be) found such pastimes about as congenial as the abominable wagons and stage-coaches by which one was forced to travel in the country west of Las Animas, Colorado. It was to be another six years before the railroads would join hands and the AT&SF was pushing fast up the approaches to the Raton Pass between Trinidad and Las Vegas. Right now it was just a long hard climb.

'We'll keep our visit here as inconspicuous as possible, Mr Dempsey,' Grant said to his aide. The young soldier saluted, and went out. Grant looked out at the unlovely huddle of railroad shanties and rubbed his hands together. He was as bored with the gentlemen of the east as they were outraged by him, and he was frankly eager to spend some time with his own kind again. Professional soldiers were a special breed. Grant loved them all like brothers.

This campaign trail he was now blazing was in many ways an historic one. The newspapers back east had made much capital of the fact that an American President was actually going to follow the route of the old pioneers down the Santa Fé Trail. He had made major speeches along the way, and smiled, recalling the ovation he had received at St Louis. Kansas City had turned out with flags and bunting to greet him, and there had been a very agreeable dinner at Fort Larned that had developed into a long and heated discussion of military tactics and policy which had gone on into the early hours of the morning.

Grant smiled. He was looking forward to some of the stops along the route that lay ahead through the mountains. He took a boyish delight in throwing his staff into confusion by making side trips to destinations they had not built into his itinerary. Well, dammit, he thought: a President has to have some fun, too.

'The escort has arrived, sir,' his aide said, entering the compartment. 'Major Godwin presents his compliments.'

'Have him come in,' Grant said, waving his cigar.

After a few minutes there was a knock on the door and a short, slimly built man with greying hair came in, his uniform dusty but correct, saluting with a smart snap that made Grant smile with pleasure.

'At ease, Major,' he said. 'Take a seat.'

The Major sat down stiffly, his eyes wide at the opulence of Grant's railroad carriage.

'Only way to travel,' Grant smiled. 'Pity we can't go all the way in it.'

'Yes, sir,' the Major said. 'I wouldn't mind going the rest of the way in this myself. It'll be,' he added hesitantly, 'a bit rougher riding from here on in, I'm afraid.'

'Don't fret yourself, laddie,' boomed Grant.

'I'm looking forward to the journey. What have you got for me?'

'We brought two ambulances, Mister President,' the soldier said. 'Good teams. A light escort, as specified.'

'Right, right,' Grant said. 'Don't want to look like an expedition. What's our route?'

'It's a fairly straightforward one, Mister President,' Godwin said. 'From here we follow the old Trail up to Trinidad. You are making a speech at a dinner given in your honour by the Friends of the Republican Party of Colorado in the Baca House . . .'

'Speeches,' grumbled Grant. There was a world of feeling in the word.

'Yes, sir,' Godwin said. 'From Trinidad we head down through the Raton to Fort Union. I am commanded by my superior, Colonel Whitenfield, to present his compliments, and to extend an invitation to dine with the officers of Fort Union upon your arrival there.'

'Fine, fine,' nodded Grant. 'May want to make a detour on the way, though.'

'Sir?' Godwin looked dismayed.

'Cimarron, boy, Cimarron,' Grant said. 'One of the best chefs I ever had opened an hotel there. The St James. Ought to get a decent meal off Henry, wouldn't you think?'

Godwin remained silent, his face a study in embarrassed confusion.

131

'Well, boy, what is it?' Grant barked. 'Speak up, speak up!'

'Ah, begging the President's pardon,' Godwin managed. 'But the Cimarron. The St James. It – uh – it hasn't the best reputation, sir, I mean. There have been . . . fights. Shootings.'

'Killings, you mean?' Grant said, a smile spreading across his bearded face. 'Good, good. Liven things up.'

'Yes, sir, Mister President,' Godwin said. He'd let Grant's staff handle that one. If he got back to Fort Union and told that fat fool Whitenfield that he'd let Grant go rummaging around Cimarron, where a man could get shot for spitting carelessly, his own commission wouldn't be worth the parchment it was printed on.

Grant stood up, ending the interview.

'Get your men ready, Major,' he said. 'We'll leave as soon as the baggage is stowed aboard the ambulances. Have you got a horse for me?'

Godwin's mouth fell open slightly.

'You wish to ride, Mister President?' he managed.

'Goddammit, boy, what else would I want a horse for?'

'I'd be honoured if you would accept the use of my horse, sir,' Godwin said, recovering. 'I'll put one of the men in an ambulance with your staff.'

'Good.' Grant nodded, and the younger man went out. He watched the soldier go, with a smile touching his lips. They must think I've forgotten how to fork a goddammed horse, he thought. That's what being a politician does for you. Thirty-odd years in the Army and they think you forget how to ride just because you sit in a fat chair in the White House. By God, he thought, I might just show them a thing or two before this trip is over. He lit another cigar and started putting his papers together.

Denniston rode at the head of his column, a smile on his lips. It was happening. Everything he had planned, organised, built for, coming finally to its preordained conclusion. He looked over his shoulder at the men behind him. Cannon fodder, he thought. Everyone of them would be either dead or a criminal whose only end would be the gallows. He knew his history: the conspirators who had murdered Lincoln had been hunted down at enormous cost to the young Republic, but hunted down one by one they had been – and then hanged. The Government had taken no chances. Nor would it this time. There was no question but that the attack which he, Denniston, would lead would bring about the greatest manhunt in the history of the United States, and he relished the thought. His name would live in history along with Grant's, locked together at the moment of Grant's death, so that whenever men spoke of one they would automatically speak of the other.

The irony of it, the full truthful justness of that fact, made Denniston smile again. Justice, indeed, he told himself. He had no illusions about his own future. As soon as he knew Grant was dead – and his soul longed to be the instrument, the actual visitor of that death – he would head for Denver. Long, long ago he had placed funds in a bank there, together with documents and letters which established a new identity for him. With the money and the new identity, he could head for San Francisco and there take a ship to England. In England he would buy a farm somewhere, perhaps in the rolling hills of Surrey, not too far from the pleasures of the metropolis, and spend the rest of his days in quiet peace among the incurious British. If his plan failed, he would kill himself. He did not think suicide dishonourable; he knew that in their hearts most soldiers felt as he did. The Paladins of old, the Crusaders, the Samurai of Japan, all had a code in which dishonour equalled death, either death in battle facing an enemy, or death by one's own hand in the sight of whatever God a man worshipped. Denniston had fled only once from death. He knew he would never do so again.

Now the long march was almost over.

He had led his men across the mountain trails between Laughlin and Tinaja Peaks, the long cavalcade snaking and twisting its way though the

134

desolate awesome mountain country and then up around the western edge of Raton Mesa, down the long falling slope of the sierras until they came to the tumbling, rushing waters in the gorge of the Picketwire River, running north and westwards to Las Animas.

Around them and above them the mighty peaks towered. The wind moaned in the canyons, and the men shivered in the cold of the high altitudes. *Rio de Las Animas en Purgatorio* – river of souls in Purgatory – Denniston rolled the words around his tongue. How beautifully apt it was! How just – the word kept coming back to him when he thought of the culmination of his plans. It was fated to be.

Now they were approaching their final camp. Tomorrow, if all went as expected, Grant's train would reach the end of the AT&SF line at Las Animas. By that time, Denniston's vedettes would be in place, stationed strategically all along the possible routes that the Presidential caravan might take, runners with the best horses that money could buy ready to swing into the saddle and bring the information back to him.

His lip curled as he thought how cheaply, and how easily, he had bought the young Major at Fort Union who had provided him with so much vital information. The robberies, the ambush of the wagon train, had all been made possible by information provided by the soldier, and the more deaths Denniston's men had wrought, the deeper into Denniston's toils the soldier fell. Finally, he had managed to get the one document which made the final coup possible. He had not, of course, known why Denniston wanted it. It was simply one piece of information among a number which he was told to get. Denniston, like many other fanatics, worked very much on the need to know principle. The Presidential itinerary was a simple one. He was speechmaking across country: St Louis, Kansas City, Trinidad, Santa Fé. There was a Republican Convention in Santa Fé at which he would naturally be expected to appear, and Grant was wasting no chance of capitalising on the journey.

Denniston had considered the possibility of an assassination by sniper at the Convention and discarded it. He wanted Grant to know why he was dying. And the military ambush which he, Denniston, was planning to effect would be a fitting way for Grant to go. Again the word justice occurred to him. Death by ambush in the canyon of the river of lost souls. Just, indeed. Denniston's face was set and cold. He looked out over the tumbled land like an eagle seeking prey.

CHAPTER
FOURTEEN

Angel watched them set their trap.

Although he was no military strategist, he could not help but admire the effectiveness of Denniston's dispersion of his men. Between the chattering Packetwire and the road, at a place where the old Trail curved around and almost back upon itself as it laboured upwards into the mountains, Denniston spread his men among the trees, where they dug holes and shallow trenches, lying and mock-sighting the Winchesters and Springfields on their imaginary target in the road. At the crest of the curve itself, among tumbled boulders that frowned down on the steeply-sloping Trail, Denniston's men manhandled the spindly Gatling gun into position, its brassy snout dulled now with blacking, stacking brush and tree branches around it until it blended with the broken land, its field of fire the curve below, towards which men fired upon would unquestionably scatter. Behind and around the gun other men were scooping out shallow dugouts, rolling big rocks into position to provide cover, a further addition to the terrible scything weight of fire which the primitive machine-gun would lay down on the Trail below. The opposite side of the Trail was simply a huge mound of broken rock, boulders, sliding shale and scree, around which the Trail curled like a snake skirting a stone. Among the jumbled, faceless rocks Denniston placed the rest of his men. They merged into the scenery almost as soon as they sank down to the ground. The sum total of the dispersion was a wall of death through which no living thing could possibly go.

Angel nodded grimly. How long did he have? How far away was the quarry? Why was the President of the United States coming through this empty, forbidden place? It did not matter. What did matter now was that he find a way to head off the President, to ensure that no one entered this place of death.

It was slow going.

He could not allow himself or his tired horse to make any noise, yet he must find a way through mountain country he had never seen and get to the Trail below the ambush. His whole body ached with fatigue. He had not eaten a warm meal for three days and the stubble was thick and rasping on his unshaven chin. His clothes felt heavy and sticky with sweat.

He worked his way over northwards, always bearing west when a canyon or a coulee offered a path through the tumbling mountains. And always he kept the tumbling Picketwire on his left, wary as an antelope for vedettes from Denniston's column, leading the stumbling horse as well as he could, sometimes sliding down yards of broken stone to the edge of the indifferent river.

He almost missed the first lookout.

The man was leaning indolently against a tree, his brown shirt and pants blending with the darker greens of the pines, a brand new Winchester canted across his forearm. Angel clamped a hand over the horse's muzzle: a whinny of alarm from the animal now could give the guard all the time he needed to fire a warning shot, bringing reinforcements down the canyon from the army above. Angel went on his belly and wormed forward until he was within ten feet of the guard. The man was peering off down the Trail, his face three-quarters turned away from Angel as Angel came up off the ground in a long fast hard run, the flat-bladed throwing knife already raised as the guard heard the movement and turned, frantically trying to get the

Winchester into firing position, seeing Angel's hand drop. For the merest fraction of a second the man's eyes picked up the whickering blade and then it drove deep into his throat, smacking his head against the tree as it went straight through, killing any sound he might have made, and pinning the man momentarily to the wood behind him. Then the dying weight of the guard against the razor edge of the blade freed it slightly, and he went down in the soft pine needles without a sound, thrashing slightly for a moment, and then as still as the death which had claimed him. Angel looked about him quickly, and, spying a cordon of rocks off near the edge of the river, dragged the man down to it and unceremoniously tumbled the body behind them. Picking up the Winchester and checking to see if it was fully loaded, he unhitched the horse and went on down the gorge of the Picketwire, moving as fast as he dared, ever alert for more guards.

It was well after noon when he emerged on a bluff from which he could see far down the long straight track leading back into the wooded declivities below. The Trail was empty except for a slow-moving wagon with a six-ox team toiling its way painfully down the long miles towards Las Animas. Far off, Angel's keen eyes picked up a trace of smoke on the smudgy edge of a bluff; perhaps ten miles away. He nodded, and then pulled the horse around, swinging aboard the sweating bare back and urging the tired animal down the trail. If there were any of Denniston's men this far out of the mountains, they would not take any notice of a man going away from the ambush. He had no doubt that any lone rider or wagon team coming down the Pass would be allowed through the cordon. They were only interested in one target.

Ten minutes after Angel was brought to him and showed the President his identification, Grant took command.

Within another ten, a team of three troopers with six extra mounts was thrashing its way back towards Las Animas with special instructions, told to kill the horses if necessary. The encampment itself was on the banks of the Picketwire, where the river, wider here and slower, purled onwards towards its eventual meeting with the Arkansas. They were about ten miles off the main Trail. Grant wasted no time on preliminaries. Leaving his three political companions sitting on the steps of the army ambulance, their faces white as chalk at the thought of the ambush lying ahead of them in the mountains, Grant assembled his staff in a semi-circle around him.

'Now,' he said. Angel watched him, amazed at the enthusiasm in the man's voice. It looked as if the President was really enjoying himself. 'In thirty-six hours, or –' he took a fob watch from his waistcoat pocket, – 'roughly seven o'clock tomorrow evening, Colonel Whitenhouse will lead a force of picked men down the pass to attack this renegade Denniston from the rear. At the same time, we – reinforced by the men I have sent for from Las Animas – will go into the, ah, lion's jaws. Although with one small difference: we shall be ready for him.'

Major Godwin stepped forward. His face was ashen, the stricken visage of a man who had just been told he has an incurable disease.

'But Mister President,' he said, 'Denniston has a Gatling gun, enormous firepower up there. We'll be cut to ribbons.'

Grant smiled. 'I doubt that, Mister,' he said. 'I've requisitioned explosives from the railroad at Animas. I propose to take that renegade bastard with a variation on the theme of the wooden horse of Troy.'

'Sir?' said Godwin.

'Later, Mister, later. Gentlemen, Mister Angel believes – and I concur – that we are probably being watched. Therefore I propose that we proceed on our way, going perhaps a lot more slowly than we might heretofore have done. We shall camp at the foot of the mountains tonight, and take a very late breakfast. We might even go fishing,' he grinned, his yellow teeth showing

142

under the bristling beard. 'But we shall not go into the pass until late afternoon, timing our arrival there for as close to six-thirty as possible. Mister Angel – perhaps you could draw us a rough map of the ambush, and the approaches to it?'

Angel smoothed out the sandy dirt and with a stick traced the major features of the Trail as it curved through the timbered rocks where the ambush was planned. Grant nodded, listening carefully, asking questions occasionally. Godwin watched it all in silence, his eyes ever wary, flickering from Angel to Grant and then out towards the mountains, never still. Grant noticed the young soldier's nervousness but dismissed it as no more than that. Angel noticed it, too. They went on talking long into the afternoon as Grant made suggestions, Angel adding other ideas, varying them constantly until they came up with the right way to do what Grant had in mind. Grant's eyes sparkled with anticipation and Frank Angel found himself warming to the short, blunt-spoken man. Grant might not have held command for many years, but he had forgotten little about soldiering. It was a pleasure to do business with him, and Angel found himself being caught up in the President's confident enthusiasm.

Later that night they camped in a box canyon at the foot of the mountains, the campfires heaped high with brush and the men encouraged to get a singsong going. In truth, they felt as little like singing as any soldier does who knows the morrow may see him dead, but Grant walked around the encampment, stopping here and there to talk to a trooper, asking questions about their homes, their families.

Later, he sent for Angel, who went to the ambulance in which Grant was to sleep and knocked on the door. He heard the gruff voice bid him enter.

Grant was sitting upon the slatted seat which would later be his bed. He gestured with the whiskey bottle in his hand towards a glass which Frank Angel picked up and held out. Grant poured him a man-sized drink and raised his glass.

'I haven't thanked you, Frank,' he said quietly.

'No need of that, Mister President,' Angel said.

'Probably not,' Grant huffed. 'But thank you, anyway. Now tell me about this man Denniston.'

So Angel sat there in the dark ambulance and told the President the story of Denniston's dismissal from the Army. When he had finished, Grant nodded.

'I remember it now,' he said quietly. 'I was stupid, sentimental. Overrode a recommendation to have the man shot. I had doubts that he had run from the Johnny Rebs the way his officers said. Always felt that it was nearer a mutiny than anything. Denniston was a martinet. Treated his men like dirt. Always took the position most likely to be under heavy fire. A glory hunter. We've got a few in the Army. Trouble, every one of them. I'm foolish about it, I suppose. Hate to see a good soldier ruined by a hasty decision. Cause me more pain before I die, I shouldn't wonder.'

'What exactly happened, sir?'

'Denniston, you mean? Can't remember the details exactly. He took a forward position, tried to carry a redoubt that was impossibly well-defended. Couldn't be done. Stood there trying to whip his men into the fight with the flat of his sabre, and when they ran he was left alone. Johnny Rebs came out to get him and the man turned tail and ran. Happened before. Unfortunately for Denniston, he ran smack into the arms of General Thomas, who was advancing with reinforcements to relieve him. Nothing Thomas could do.'

Angel nodded. As Grant had said, it had happened before, and no one the wiser many times. Denniston had suffered an extreme penalty for that one lapse. It was no wonder that the hatred for Grant had rankled all those years, festering until it became a mad ambition, revenge, revenge, revenge the only force in the twisted mind.

He bade the President goodnight and went out

into the night. The stars wheeled in their courses over the high terrain. Somewhere a horse whickered. He stood for a long time looking up at the mountains.

Hours later, he slept.

CHAPTER FIFTEEN

Late in the afternoon the two ambulances toiled up the long mountain road. It was one of those days you sometimes get in the high country, hot and still, the sky a brazen white without a cloud anywhere and only the soft sigh of the everpresent breeze to cool the sweating bodies of the troopers riding escort. Denniston's vedettes had signalled the advance of the Presidential caravan, their prearranged Morse signals winking from the high points. If the troopers escorting the ambulances saw them, they gave no sign.

Denniston was waiting as he had waited for almost two days, clamping down upon the burning impatience that consumed him. He knew Grant's reputation for dawdling, knew the man would feel it a challenge to alter any timetable with which he was presented; the faintest touch of cold unease had once come to Denniston in the bleak cool of the mountain night and he had wondered, wondered. But no. Godwin would

147

have sent word to him if there had been any change of plan, any possibility that the final dénouement was to be denied him. And none had come. What Denniston could not know was that Frank Angel had, without ever seeming to do so, kept ever close to the young major, always around when Godwin thought, for once, that he might be able to sneak away from the encampment. Godwin had cursed the Justice Department man silently many times, but it was no use his trying to warn Denniston in any way. That was exactly what Angel was waiting for – one man to try to leave the column. He would know then. And there was something in Angel's cold eyes that warned Godwin he would never deliver his message if he tried. And so he had remained close to his men, busying himself unnecessarily, always hopeful that the chance which had never come might present itself.

Up the long, winding road the wagons toiled. The Army mules had their ears laid back, their backs wet with sweat as they lunged against the traces, hauling the ambulances over the rocky road, the vehicles swaying dangerously on the deep ruts scoured into the Trail by generations of heavy-laden Conestogas.

Frank Angel rode in the rear of the procession, a bearded trooper alongside him. The trooper's eyes constantly moved across the rocky bluffs on either side of the trail, ever alert for some movement, some indication that they were closing in on their destination.

'Goddammit, Angel,' the trooper said, 'why can't I have a cigar?'

'Mr President, you'd be the first cavalryman in the history of the Army who was allowed to smoke while escorting the President of the United States. No go. Sorry.'

'All right, all right,' grumbled Grant. 'Beats me how you can smoke one and I can't, that's all.'

Angel grinned. 'I'm a civilian, remember?'

They were on a fairly straight stretch of the trail now, and Angel spurred the horse up alongside the second ambulance, standing in the saddle to see ahead. The troopers in the van, led by Godwin, were just approaching a left-hand bend. Beyond it and above them the road straightened up and then turned almost on itself to the right. There was a huge mound of rocks and boulders screened by patches of brush where the trail swung, and on the river side, heavy pines screened the roadside.

Angel nodded, falling back alongside Grant.

'This it?' Grant asked. His face was set and tight. He shifted impatiently in the McClellan.

'This is it,' Angel confirmed.

'Carry on, Mister Angel,' Grant said curtly. 'Good luck.'

'Thanks,' Angel said. He put his heels into the horse's ribs and kicked it to a run, coming up alongside Godwin. He had his Stetson tugged down well over his eyes and hunched his shoulders. If Denniston was up there with field-glasses – and he surely was – Angel didn't want him recognising the man he thought long since executed in the compound.

'Fall back nice and easy, now,' Angel said quietly to the soldiers flanking him, letting his horse make its own pace. 'Let the front ambulance come up on you a little. That's it, that's fine. Easy, now.'

The driver of the leading ambulance winked at Angel as he came level, his features tight with anticipation. They were twenty, thirty yards from the bend, now, and that was when Angel yelled 'GO!'

The driver of the ambulance laid the whip across the backs of the astonished mules, which bared their teeth in shock and lunged against the traces, actually starting to run up the steep slope as the troopers on both sides of the ambulance scattered, falling sideways out of their saddles, rifles in hand, scrabbling to find any cover they could. The driver of the ambulance leaped to one side, landing running, then falling, crashing into the trees, his body tumbling down to the edge of the rushing river as the ambulance clattered into the bend, the short fuse to which Angel had touched his cigar sputtering beneath the seat. The mules charged into the corner with no hope at all of negotiating it, pulling back and making the ambulance swing off to the left hand side of the track, rolling on top of the hidden riflemen in the trees there and then suddenly exploding, detonating with a cracking boom that hurled splinters and tattered things that might have once been parts of men high in a bloody mêlée.

Up on the rise overlooking the curve Denniston screamed orders to his men, the Gatling gun starting to pump shells down on to the road, the explosions chattering like some enormous beast as the gunner wound the crank handle. Great gouts of earth and rock smashed upwards as the line of shells marched down the road, dropping the lead mules of the second wagon, lifting upwards, shredding the woodwork of the conveyance, tearing great chunks of it that whickered towards the crouching, flinching men. Now the riflemen on the mound in the centre of the curve opened up, laying down a flat screen of fire that ripped the thin slatted sides of the Army ambulance into smithereens and finally, as Angel had expected, one of them hit the explosives inside and the wagon went up with a roar, a yellow tongue of flame licking twenty feet high as the whirling pieces of timber, wagon bed, canvas, metal, dead mule, filled the sky with heavy rain.

Now the Gatling gun had nothing to shoot at because a dense cloud of black smoke hung over the whole curve, yet still Denniston screamed at his gunner and still the man cranked the handle, pouring an endless hail of shells into the churning mess on the road below. Through the smashing roll of firing, the troopers were getting the distance from their position at the side of the road, their slugs whacking great chunks off the rocks in the central mound. Then Angel, belly-down in the trees between the river and the road, heard the clear, lovely sound of a cavalry bugle and over the top of the rise, guidons flying, came a double rank of United States Cavalry.

Now the troopers under Angel's position raised a cheer and fired a volley into the air, and up the Trail from their position away behind the President's caravan came a motley crowd of railroad men; steel men and gandy dancers, track layers, navvies, ferried up the side of the pass in big supply wagons with canvas tops, every one of them armed with repeating rifles, spreading like a swarm of ants behind the men entrenched there and showing no one an ounce of mercy.

The troopers in the trees got to their feet now, racing along behind Major Godwin, who ran flat out ahead of them towards the bluff on which Denniston stood, the Gatling gun still churning out its rain of death on the milling figures below. It mattered nothing to Denniston whose men the terrible Gatling gun shells killed. No man down there was his friend.

'Shoot, shoot, shoot, shoot!' he screamed monotonously on and on, knowing that he had been tricked, realising that Grant was not there, that the whole thing had failed. The soldiers below kept on coming and now the troopers coming over the top of the rise were charging into the mêlée. One detachment veered to the right, led by a young lieutenant with corn yellow hair flying in the wind of his gallop, his arm outstretched, a Colt's revolver glinting in the sun.

Denniston saw the soldier fire and felt the wind of the bullet on his cheek as he screamed at his men to swing the Gatling gun around to face this new threat. The noise and confusion were too intense: his men did not hear him. And then the cavalrymen were on them. The young lieutenant launched himself from the back of his horse on to the shoulders of the man operating the crank handle of the Gatling, feeling the man beneath his flying weight.

Denniston looked right, left, rapidly seeking an escape route. The road leading towards Trinidad was clear now, the last trooper embroiled in the fighting going on in the road and alongside it. Shots whistled everywhere. Men were sprawled brokenly on both sides of the road, some of them in the dark blue of the US Army. Denniston edged around two men fighting on the ground, saw a trooper coming at him in the same instant and shot the man in the face. The soldier went down in a welter of spraying blood and brains as

Denniston ran hard and fast towards the left hand side of the road where trees came almost to the very roadside itself. Once in the tall timber he would have a chance. All he had to do was get across one high rocky ridge that loomed in front of him and he would be out of sight. He ran towards it with manical intensity, his only thought to get over it and away.

He actually had his hands on the rock when a remembered voice cut through the white panic in his brain.

'Don't say you're leaving just when the party's getting interesting, Colonel?'

He whirled around, pure disbelief on his face.

'You!' he choked.

'Me, indeed,' said President Grant. 'And Mr Angel you also know.'

Denniston took it all in. Below and behind the two men in front of him the firing had stopped. The soldiers were herding together a half-dozen or so sullen survivors, their hands raised above their heads as the troopers poked them together with rifle barrels none too gently. There were bodies sprawled everywhere in the hot sun, some of them in Army blue, many more not. The last faint wisps of powder smoke drifted away and the hot sun shone down forgivingly, long shadows darkening the bloodstained trail.

It was all over. Denniston frowned. How could it be all over? Then his eyes focused on the two men in front of him and his mind snapped. There are medical terms to describe that exact occurrence. It can be caused by a shock beyond the powers of the brain to reject. On other occasions it is caused by a rush of rage so intense that inside the delicate frontal lobes small nerve cells break apart, and on still others it is a complete loss of all normal control.

Whatever it was, Denniston felt it go, just as the two men standing in front of him saw the bright glare that flickered to Denniston's eyes.

There was a pure bright blinding light behind Denniston's eyes and he knew finally that he was invulnerable, invincible. He knew too that because he was all these things his mortal enemy was delivered into his hands. All he could see in the whole astonishing bright world he now lived in was Ulysses S. Grant, awaiting his punishment, his execution, as the droning sound of the 'Rogues' March' filled Denniston's mind and he lifted the gun out of its closed-top holster, savouring the moment he would pull the trigger. Somewhere in another part of the mind he heard Angel shout something, but whatever it was had no meaning, no place in this perfect world, so he ignored it, lifting the Navy Colt and cocking it deliberately, the triple click as loud as thunder. He felt as if he were on the top of some snow-covered peak high in the mountains, alone, perfected. And he felt no pain at all when Angel shot him dead.

CHAPTER SIXTEEN

Grant's speech at the Santa Fé Convention was, they read, tremendous. 'The President,' Angel read aloud, 'received a standing ovation lasting more than ten minutes, and many of those present were not ashamed to be seen wiping tears from their eyes.'

'It actually says that?' Wells asked.

'Right here,' Angel said, pointing to the paragraph in the *Optic*.

'Doesn't sound like the President Grant we all got to know and love,' said Lieutenant Philip Evans. He was in the bed next to Wells, recuperating from a flesh wound he had received in the fighting at the pass, ten days before.

Grant had come down from the mountains like a grizzly with a sore head. Colonel Whitenfield had been ordered to put an expedition into the field immediately, to ride up into the mountains above Kiowa and wipe out whatever remained of the Denniston compound. They had found the place deserted except for buzzards picking on what was left of the men Angel had killed, and burned it to the ground.

Angel had telegraphed his advance report to Washington, advising them that Wells, although wounded, was not dead. The day before Grant left for Santa Fé, he had sent for Angel.

He had gone into the officers' quarters in the big adobe on the north side of the sprawling fort and found Grant sitting there, whiskey at his elbow, cigar stuck into his face at the old jaunty angle.

'Wanted to thank you,' Grant began with grace. 'Officially.'

Angel thanked him and Grant waved him to a chair.

'Sit down, sit down,' he said testily. 'Don't be so hard to get.' He got up and walked around the desk, sitting on the edge and stabbing his cigar at Angel.

'Want you on my personal staff,' he said abruptly. 'Like your style, Angel.'

'Thank you, Mister President,' Angel said. 'But—'

'But me no buts, boy,' the President said. 'I'll talk to the Attorney General about it. Dammit, I'll order him to transfer you to me. One of the nice things about being President.' He peered at Angel. 'Well, what do you say, man?'

'With respect, Mister President,' Angel said. 'I'd prefer to stay where I am. I think it would be better.'

'Can't go along with that, Angel,' Grant said, getting off the desk and going back to his chair. 'I need men like you around me. God! I can still see that man pointing that gun at me.'

'I don't think he really knew what he was doing, sir,' Angel said.

'Maybe, maybe,' Grant said, 'but I stood there hypnotised. I'll never laugh at anyone who tells me about birds and snakes again, I assure you. Now, about that job. Say you'll take it.'

'No, sir,' Angel said. 'I can't do that.'

'Can't?' Grant erupted. 'Can't do what the President of the United States tells you to do?'

'No, sir,' Angel said, straight faced.

'You better come up with a damned good reason, boy!' warned Grant. 'A damned good reason.'

Angel nodded. 'I got one,' he said. 'You see, Mister President – I'm a Democrat.'

Grant looked at him for a long, long moment, trying hard to hold the scowl on his bearded face. It was no use. The laughter bubbled up and spread all over it, and he threw back his head and shouted his laughter so loud that the orderly opened the door and poked in his head to make sure all was well.

'What is it?' said Grant, his shoulders heaving.

'Everything in order, Mister President, sir?' the sergeant said.

'Yes,' wheezed Grant. 'Fine. Fine. Mister Angel is a Democrat, you see.'

The clerk looked at Angel, then back at Grant.

'Oh, yes, Mister President, I see,' he said, retreating into his own office and tapping his head significantly in response to the inquiring look of the other orderly sergeant, who nodded. Everyone knew that Grant was mad. Drank some, too, they said.

In the hospital, Angel stood up and stretched.

'How long before you're fit to travel?' he asked Wells.

'Month, six weeks, they tell me,' Wells grinned. 'I wouldn't be surprised if it took longer.'

'You want me to tell the Old Man that?'

'Well, Frank,' Wells bcamed, unashamed, 'it'd come so much better from you – you being a hero, and getting that special commendation from the President, like. You know, you've got clout now.'

'Oh, sure,' Angel said. 'Sure.'

'Never know,' Wells said teasingly. 'The Old Man might even let you take that lovely secretary of his out to dinner.'

'She pretty, Gus?' Evans asked from the other bed.

Wells pursed his lips and made one of those

159

movements with both hands that men make to indicate loveliness.

'Ahah,' Evans said. 'Now we know why Frank's in such a hurry to get back east.'

Angel said something rude and turned to leave. As he did, he caught Wells' eye and grinned.

'See you at the May Ball,' he said.

'I'll be there,' Wells promised. 'And I'll be dancing.'

Angel nodded and went out of there. He got his horse, standing ready with his bedroll strapped behind the saddle. He swung aboard and took one last look at Fort Union. Then without regret he kicked the horse into a canter and rode out through the gates on to the trail leading up into the mountains. If anyone had seen him just then they might have been surprised, for he was smiling.

He knew just the place he could take her.